BLAZING UPHEAVAL

based on a true story

KAREN CHARLES

ISBN: 979-8-35095-950-5

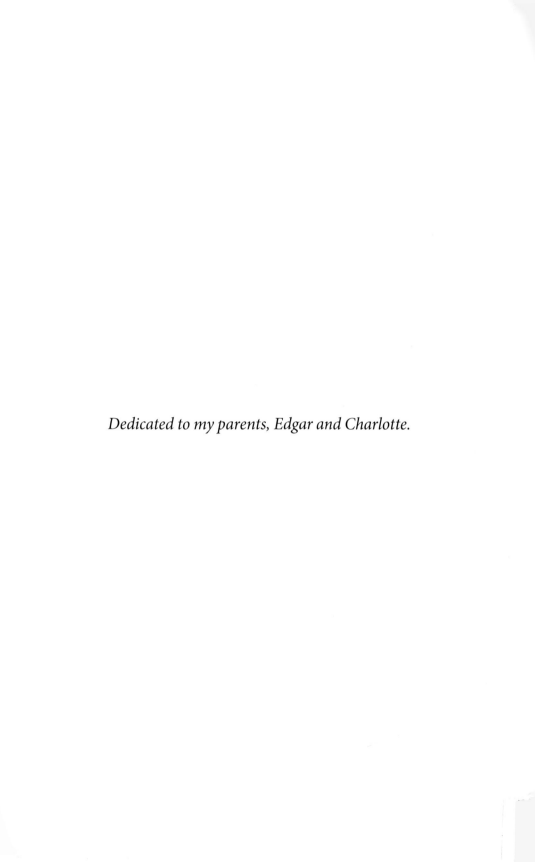

Dedicated to my parents, Edgar and Charlotte.

Revenge is like a rolling stone, which, when a man hath forced up a hill, will return upon him with a greater violence and break those bones whose sinews gave it motion.

JEREMY TAYLOR

CHAPTER ONE

TIFFANY GLANCED OUT OF THE bank of the windows along the side of her first-grade classroom. Ashes rained down as though the heavens were on fire, creating an ominous darkness. Anxiety gripped her! What was burning? The fire alarm had not sounded at school.

Most parents heeded the warning of unrest in the community and kept their children at home. Out of the six students, who showed up that day in Tiffany's class, only Orlando remained. He sat in his seat, engrossed in a book with stunning marine-life photography. He was unaware of the chaos outside.

The principal of Leo Politi Elementary School, bordering Koreatown in Los Angeles, sent an urgent request for parents to pick up their children immediately. In any emergency, teachers could not leave until all their students had left the campus.

The ringing phone on Tiffany's desk startled them both. "Hello," she answered, remaining calm.

"Bring Orlando to the office. His mom was called. She must have rolled over and gone back to sleep. The principal will supervise him until she gets here. It would be best if you left, NOW!" explained the school secretary.

"Orlando, get your backpack. We're going to the office," Tiffany instructed. She grabbed her heavy school bag and purse.

The sight, upon stepping outside onto the walkway, was terribly shocking. The cool morning air was filled with orchid-gray billows of swirling smoke. The acrid smell stung her nostrils. Clasping Orlando's hand, they rushed to the office, sheltered on the covered sidewalks. Another student also waited in the office. He cried softly in a corner chair. The principal and the vice-principal would wait for their parents to pick them up while the secretary and Tiffany headed home. A somber principal hurried them to the staff parking lot, unlocking the gate. He reluctantly let them out into a hellish nightmare of rioting, arson, looting, and murder!

The night before, the Los Angeles School District instructed the teachers to come to school as usual if the area looked calm. Coming from the San Fernando Valley, Tiffany took the Olympic Boulevard exit off the CA-110 freeway. Driving down the fourteen blocks to Leo Politi Elementary, the streets were quiet. She breathed a sigh of relief. Little did Tiffany realize that, within three hours, the gates of hell would break loose.

The day before, April 29, 1992, at the Simi Valley Court House, a jury acquitted all four of the LAPD officers who assaulted a Black man named Rodney King. During the early morning hours of March 3, 1991, after a night of binge drinking, King and some friends were speeding down the Foothill Freeway. He was erratically driving his 1987 Hyundai when two California Highway Patrol officers spotted them. They gave chase but could not force him to stop. King panicked not wanting to be arrested while intoxicated, in case it was a parole violation. Speeding off the freeway, he tried to elude his pursuers through residential neighborhoods. Soon, Los Angeles Police Department patrol cars and a police helicopter joined the chase. They pinned him down and ordered King and his two friends out of the car.

When Rodney King emerged from the car, the officers said he acted "peculiarly," waving to the helicopter and stomping his feet. They tasered him and the order was given to subdue him.

Unknown to the officers, a tenant in a nearby apartment captured the next seventy-nine seconds, recording King's resistance. The officers responded by beating him with their batons and kicking him thirty times. Later, when a pulverized King was taken to the hospital, he was diagnosed with a broken ankle, a broken facial bone, and multiple lacerations.

The tenant took his videotape to a local television station. They broadcast the graphic display of police brutality, sparking outrage in the Black community.

Now, with the acquittal of the officers who assaulted Rodney King, a group gathered at the intersection of Florence and Normandie Avenues in Los Angeles. Emotions ran high. A White truck driver, Reginald Denny, stopped his truck at the traffic light at that intersection. A group dragged him out of his truck and beat him. Anger was now at the boiling point, ready for a catastrophic, deadly explosion the city would never forget.

CHAPTER TWO

T IFFANY GRIPPED THE STEERING WHEEL of her silver metallic Honda Accord. She said a quick prayer as she exited through the gate of the school parking lot. Her knuckles turned white. Chaos erupted outside her car. The city of Los Angeles was consumed by anarchy. Rioters rampaged through the streets. Emotional Contagion had taken over. Anger, frustration, and excitement were intensifying. It spread among individuals. Powerful emotions caused an escalation in violence, creating a domino effect. Soon they lost control, leading to impulsive and irrational behaviors.

Looting, fires, gunshots, and the threat of murder were the grim backdrop against which Tiffany navigated her way to the safety of the freeway, fourteen blocks away. Her heart pounded with fear and adrenaline. She took deep breaths, pausing to muster her courage. Peering down the street that she took every day to the freeway entrance paralyzed her with dread. The street was a mass of people carrying electronics looted from stores. Flames roared from a Thrifty Drug. With terror, she realized she must avoid the violence of the thoroughfares.

Instead, Tiffany decided to take alternate routes, weaving through side streets and alleys. She hoped to stay clear of the worst of the turmoil. She did not know the area well but could depend on her keen sense of direction to keep herself heading toward the freeway, her only escape.

Tiffany's tires screeched as she accelerated away from the rioters, who seemed to emerge from every corner. Her heart raced as she skillfully maneuvered around burning barricades, her sharp blue eyes darting from one dangerous scene to another. Sweat dripped down her brow. Her reddish-blond hair stuck to her wet cheeks as she navigated through the maze of debris and broken glass. Her hyperawareness kept her acutely attuned to potential threats and obstacles. Flames shot out from the empty store windows, casting an eerie glow on the streets. The city transformed into a war zone. Gunshots echoed nearby, sending shivers down Tiffany's spine. She saw Korean shopkeepers up on their balconies brandishing threatening weapons, trying to protect their stores.

Tiffany knew that time was of the essence if she was to survive. Looters scurried like rats across the streets, ducking into stores, grabbing all they could hold in their arms. Cars overflowed, being stuffed with any goods they could carry. People carted cases of beer from Tom's Liquor and Deli. Tiffany pressed the accelerator, her car darting through narrow gaps, avoiding collisions with other panicked drivers. Her ability to navigate through this pandemonium, with speed and precision, could save her life.

As Tiffany rounded a corner, a crowd of rioters spilled onto the street—a frenzied, violent mob. Her heart sank. She couldn't turn back. She edged forward, honking her horn in a desperate attempt to create a path. The mob shifted, distracted by the commotion. Tiffany spotted a clear gap on the sidewalk. Clutching the steering wheel with trembling hands, she swerved, seizing the opportunity. She darted through, missing a fire hydrant, amid shouts and curses. Panic consumed her thoughts. She might not find a way out of this dangerous area!

With renewed focus, her heart pounding against her ribcage, Tiffany emerged from the fray. She realized she was only a few blocks from the freeway, her haven of safety. She pressed the gas pedal, her car surging ahead with newfound urgency.

Tiffany came to an abrupt stop at the red light at the intersection where she would make a left turn onto the freeway entrance. Loud yelling frightened her. Three men surrounded her car. They bounced it up and down. Alarm gripped her racing heart as she understood the hatred in their eyes. They pulled on the locked doors. They pounded on the windows. She felt shock and disbelief as she realized the rioters wanted to harm her! She was helpless! She was trapped!

Tiffany heard the loud screeching of tires. A pickup truck stopped in the middle of the intersection in front of her. Four men jumped out of the truck. They raced toward her car, shouting at the men bashing it. The three menacing men whipped around, startled. They prepared to defend themselves. As they all fought, two of the three men attacking her car, hit the pavement! The last one spun around to run but a powerful blow sent him flying through the broken window of a burning store.

Someone knocked on Tiffany's car window. Petrified, she looked up at a vaguely familiar face. He waved her through the intersection toward the freeway entrance. Tiffany did not hesitate. She raced onto the freeway. Tears streamed down her face. She had defied the odds and escaped the chaos that threatened to consume her, leaving behind the burning city and the turmoil that gripped it. The distant sounds of the police and fire truck sirens faded away as Tiffany headed for the San Fernando Valley, home.

CHAPTER THREE

Tiffany turned into her Northridge neighborhood in the San Fernando Valley, twenty-eight miles away from Leo Politi Elementary. Relief and happiness washed over her when she reached her familiar street, fringed with mature Jacaranda trees. Soon they would burst with clouds of purple flowers beautifying their front yards. She turned into her driveway, parked, and turned off the car. She did not stir for a while, just sat, trying to collect herself. Noting the time, her two kids were still at school and her husband, Bill, would be at work. Uneasiness spread through Tiffany's thoughts. Did that truly happen? Did I drive through a riot and survive? Am I safe now sitting in my car in the driveway? Are my kids safe at school?

A tapping on Tiffany's car window startled her back from her reverie.

Bill opened the door. "You're home!" he exclaimed.

"Yes, I'm home!" she sighed, exiting the car.

Tiffany fell into the safety of his arms. Tears soaked Bill's neck as she sobbed, her body heaving against his.

Calming a little she asked, "You're home early?"

"I called your school. They said you left two hours before so I came home to wait for you. A headache came on also," he informed her.

"I'm glad you're here! Did you take something for your headache?"

"Yes." With his strong arm around Tiffany's shoulders, they walked into their home.

"I could use a hot shower and change into something comfortable," she said.

"I'll make some ice tea," he offered. "We can just relax."

Soon Tiffany appeared in a comfortable tropical caftan, wet hair secured back in a ponytail. Bill led her to their cozy, patio-seating area by the shimmering pool where a pitcher of sweet raspberry tea waited with chilled glasses. They sipped their tea, unwinding, escaping into the enchantment of the tropical paradise Tiffany created in their backyard. The ugly block fence enclosing the yard now served as a canvas for a vibrant, lush tapestry of greenery and color. Towering Palm trees swayed in the breeze along with tall slender Bamboo shoots. Leaves rustled, creating a serene backdrop.

Over on one side of the yard, Tiffany planted a miniature orchard boasting dwarf citrus trees and Banana plants, showing off their vibrant hues amidst the greenery.

Tiffany wove in an array of ferns and shrubs along the fence, between the trees. Birds Nest Ferns added a touch of elegance with their feathery fronds, while the Croton shrubs showcased flamboyant red, yellow, and orange leaves.

The fragrance of Hibiscus flowers hung in the air. Their blossoms showcased Tiffany's favorite shades of pink, red, and orange.

The tropical enchantment continued by the swimming pool and patio where Palm trees, both potted and planted, lined the poolside. Around the patio, hanging baskets overflowed with cascading ferns and vibrant flowers. The effect softened with an air of relaxed elegance.

Tiffany allowed herself to be plucked away, embracing the sense of tranquility.

"I was so scared for you!" Bill admitted, interrupting the silence.

"I was scared too," Tiffany agreed. "By the time I left school, rioters stormed the streets, looting the stores and setting them on fire. I worked my way around them through alleys, driving up on sidewalks, and trying to find passable streets to the freeway."

Tiffany went silent. More remained untold but he could wait.

"I don't know how long it will be before school opens again!" she mused. "Our kids should be home soon."

The riots had not spread to the San Fernando Valley, so schools were still in session.

"Speaking of our kids, here they are," Bill jumped up. Tiffany stood as Sidney and Austin burst through the sliding doors onto the patio.

"Mom, we heard about the riots!" Sidney exclaimed. "They let us out of school early."

"I made it home!" assured Tiffany, giving them a warm hug and a kiss.

Sidney, at a petite five foot three inches tall, with sparkling blue eyes and long blond hair, was known for her bubbly personality. Austin was a quieter, tall, fourteen-year-old, athletic, strawberry-blond who took everything he did seriously. Sidney, being seventeen now, drove them back and forth to school.

"All sports and activities are canceled. We don't know when we'll be going back," Austin commented, helping himself to a glass of iced tea.

Over the ensuing days, violence, looting, and arson spread to encompass much of Los Angeles. It eventually spilled over into the San Fernando Valley. Most of the destructiveness in the Valley was quelled with arrests and strong police presence. The heaviest areas damaged were the South Central district of Los Angeles and "Koreatown," located between Black neighborhoods and Hollywood. Koreans became the eventual targets of the rioting, as minorities claimed that storeowners mistreated both Latino and Black customers.

Many uncertain and unsettling days would be ahead for this family of four, filled with the painful anticipation of danger.

CHAPTER FOUR

THINKING HOW EXHAUSTED TIFFANY MUST be, Bill suggested checking to see if any pizza places were delivering.

"I need something to do," responded Tiffany. "How about our favorite Meatloaf sandwiches!"

They all four converged on their spacious kitchen. Everyone did their job, having prepared these sandwiches many times. Dad took over the island. He cut the small yellow potatoes into half-inch wedges, peeled and thinly sliced the onions, and minced a few slices for the meat mixture.

While he prepared that, Mom gently combined beef, panko, garlic powder, chicken stock concentrate, minced onion, ketchup, salt, and pepper. Adjusting the oven racks to the top and middle positions, she set the oven to 425 degrees. Tiffany formed the beef mixture into four one-inch-tall loaves on a baking sheet, brushing the tops with more ketchup.

Bill tossed the potato wedges on a baking sheet with a drizzle of olive oil, salt, and pepper. He put them on the top rack for twenty-five minutes, then slid the meatloaves on the middle rack for twenty minutes.

Austin caramelized the onions in a pan with a large drizzle of olive oil. He added a little sugar and splashes of water until the onions caramelized into a jammy consistency. Then he added a little salt and pepper.

While Dad toasted the sourdough bread in a frying pan with butter, Sidney made their scrumptious sauce. She combined mayonnaise, horseradish paste, mustard, sugar, salt, and pepper.

When everything was ready, Tiffany spread half the bread slices with caramelized onion and the remaining slices with the sauce, saving some for dipping. Meatloaf slices fanned out over the bread with the onions. She closed the sandwiches and cut them in half. Adding the roasted potato wedges, they feasted by the azure pool, laughing at crazy stories Sidney told about kids at school.

It appeared to be a normal day with a family enjoying a meal together.

Dad always cleaned up, saying, "You mess up, I clean up!"

While he put the kitchen back in order, Tiffany slipped into the pool as she did most nights after work. The sun took the chill off the cool water temperature. It felt warm and comforting. Some of the stress dissipated as she swam her laps. Sidney and Austin jumped in when she was done, diving, and shooting balls into the pool basketball hoop. Bill joined them as the day melted into the night. The backyard transformed into a magical wonderland. Soft lights twinkled among the trees and vines, casting a gentle glow on the vibrant foliage, turning the space into an ethereal sanctuary. By ten o'clock everyone headed for their rooms.

Tiffany cuddled in bed with her head nestled into Bill's neck and shoulder. Every time she shut her eyes, menacing mobs loomed before her, fires blazed with flames licking the sky, hateful eyes threatened her, and the face of an angel appeared to rescue her. Did she know him? What happened to the three men who attacked her? They would be haunting her for many months to come! She rested her head on her pillow but thoughts of what happened that day tormented her restless night!

CHAPTER FIVE

K AYLA STOOD STARING OUT HER second-floor bedroom window, horrified at the scene unfolding in her neighborhood. Her fingers twisted a long, beautiful braid as she watched the chaos of rioters. The night before she listened to the street talk from her teenage sons and prepared for trouble.

Kayla owned a beauty salon—Twisted Crown Salon—specializing in lustrous braids. It was a welcoming space adorned with bright colors and cozy seating. Her beauty salon celebrated the art of braiding, specializing in an array of intricate braiding styles designed for Black hair. Her clients enjoyed a warm ambiance, with soft music playing in the background. A blend of earthy scents lingered in the air.

The salon's interior was adorned with stunning displays showcasing different braid patterns and hair textures, celebrating the diversity and beauty of Black hair. Kayla was a talented stylist, skilled in various braiding techniques like cornrows, box braids, twists, and much more. She worked diligently creating stunning, personalized looks for each client. Kayla's salon shelves were stocked with high-quality hair products curated for textured hair, a range of natural oils, moisturizers, and styling gels. She indulged her clients in pampering sessions and scalp massages, ensuring, not just beautiful styles, but also healthy hair practices.

There was a strong sense of community within Kayla's salon. Clients chatted and shared experiences while getting their hair done. It was a unique place from which individuals left not only with fantastic hairstyles but also with a renewed sense of confidence and pride in their cultural identity. Kayla was invited all over Los Angeles to host workshops to celebrate and educate about the beauty and significance of braiding in Black culture.

The home Kayla provided for her family was cozy and attractive, tucked away above and behind the bustling beauty salon. The living space was simple, comfortable, and homey. She organized and decorated it with photographs capturing precious family moments. Downstairs, behind the salon, a small kitchen with a table opened to a welcoming living room with comfy couches and a television where they gathered in the evening. The boys played video games while Kayla relaxed after a long day in the salon.

Despite her busy schedule, Kayla made it a point to prepare home-cooked meals when possible. Often, the boys helped out with dinner preparations. They always cleaned up.

The biggest challenge for Kayla was raising her four boys. Of the three teenagers, Jordan, seventeen, and Cameron, fifteen, were her boys. She took in Jasen, also seventeen, after his father, her brother, passed away from cancer. Then there was Martin, her six-year-old boy, who attended first grade at Leo Politi Elementary School a few blocks away. Kayla's husband, Isaiah, left them a few years ago and lived in a nearby apartment with his brother. Both worked for the Los Angeles School District.

Kayla kept Martin home from school today, anticipating trouble in the community. She had him watching cartoons, keeping him away from the shocking scenes outside the windows. The acquittal of the officers, who had beaten Rodney King, stirred pent-up anger, boiling like a kettle ready to release with a blasting whistle.

Despite all the windows and doors being tightly shut and locked the night before, Kayla smelled the pungent swirling smoke rising from burning shops and stores. She heard the kitchen door downstairs crashing open.

"Mama," Jordan yelled. "Cameron's been hurt! They took him in an aid car to the Good Samaritan Hospital on Wilshire."

Shocked, Mama yelled instructions, "Call your dad. Tell him to pick us up in the alley. We need to get to the hospital!"

They waited while Mama put together medical information to take with them to the hospital. It took an hour for their dad to arrive and another hour to make their way through the hazards in the streets. Rushing to the emergency entrance, they asked about Cameron. After checking in, and giving them his medical insurance coverage, which was through his dad's job at the school district, Kayla was allowed into his room.

The medical team assessed Cameron's burns' severity, depth, size, and locations. They checked his vital signs, making sure he was stable. The burn area was cooled with cool water to prevent further tissue damage. His clothes had been removed and intravenous fluids were administered to maintain hydration and support blood pressure. They gave him pain medication and oxygen.

A doctor noticed Kayla standing by the door. "Are you his mother?" he inquired.

"Yes!" she responded, her face etched with concern.

"He's been asking for you. Tell him you are here, but don't touch him. We need to clean the burns on his arms and body to prevent infections," explained the doctor.

Kayla walked up to the side of the bed, "Cameron, I'm here and so are your dad and brothers."

Cameron turned his head slightly. "Sorry, Mama!"

"It's okay, Sweetheart. We love you. We'll be in the waiting room," she said with a catch in her voice.

Kayla's devastated family waited until the doctor came out to update them on Cameron's condition. The next step was to reassess the severity of the burns. He might have to be transferred to a specialized burn center for further treatment and care.

Cameron slept under the influence of strong pain medications. The family seized the opportunity. They gathered around a secluded table in the far corner of the hospital cafeteria, getting sandwiches and drinks.

"Now, what happened?" demanded Mama, looking at Jordan and Jasen.

Jordan described the intensity of the angry crowds. He, Jasen, and Cameron became fueled by the hatred surrounding them. They attacked a woman's car, bouncing it up and down, and tried to open the doors and windows. A group of four men in a truck pulled up and tried to stop them. The four men slammed Jordan and Jasen to the pavement. While trying to escape, Cameron fell through a broken window into a burning store.

Everyone sat in silence. Mama held Martin close as tears coursed down his face.

"They won't get away with this!" muttered Jasen under his breath. "We're going to even the score!"

CHAPTER SIX

THE NEXT DAY, THE RIOTS raged on. The mayor of Los Angeles, Tom Bradley, called a state of emergency. Governor of California, Pete Wilson, ordered two thousand National Guard troops to the city. A city curfew was announced from sunset to sunrise, mail delivery stopped, and most residents could not go to work or school.

Feeling restless and bored, Tiffany and her family decided to ask their next-door neighbors if they could play tennis on their backyard court. They were a retired couple who rarely played anymore. They had become special friends and loved watching Tiffany's family play, cheering for the kids. Five years ago, they moved from the Seattle area to the San Fernando Valley for Bill's new job at the Northeast Valley Health Corporation at their corporate office in San Fernando. With the year-round warm weather, they had gotten family tennis lessons. Sidney and Austin were quick learners. It had been a while since the four of them played together. Everyone carried such a busy schedule. Being competitive, the games were intense. Dad and Sidney teamed up against Mom and Austin. Bill seemed off in his service game so Tiffany and Austin squeezed in a winning set. Bill and Tiffany savored this time with their kids. After another fierce set, they invited their neighbors over for barbequed hamburgers. It was a relaxing, fun time visiting with them and getting updated on their family and grandkids.

Later in the evening, after their neighbors had gone home, Tiffany told the kids about the hazardous trip to the freeway from her school, through streets filled with rioting and fires. They laughed at her story of driving up on the sidewalk, barely missing the fire hydrant. It felt good to laugh but she still had not mentioned the attack!

The rioting raged on for five days. Residents set fires and looted and destroyed liquor stores, grocery stores, retail shops, and fast-food restaurants. Light-skinned motorists, both White and Latino, were targeted, pulled out of their cars, and beaten. There ended up being more than fifty riot-related deaths, two thousand people injured, and nearly six thousand looters and arsonists arrested. More than one thousand buildings were damaged or destroyed, and approximately two thousand Korean-run businesses were damaged. The city curfew was lifted on May 4. Most schools, banks, and businesses reopened.

During these restrictive days, Bill and Tiffany focused on relaxing in the pool, reading, and catching up on work-related paperwork. Sidney worked on a term paper assignment and Austin did his homework. They spent time in the yard helping each other practice Sidney's volleyball skills and Austin's soccer skills. He played the goalkeeper for his team, being tall with a long reach and quick reflexes. Sidney would kick the soccer ball to him so he could practice the catches and his footwork.

Tiffany knew she needed to cope with the stress from her traumatic experience. Maybe, eventually, she would have to seek professional help. For now, she had support from her family. She made herself eat a balanced diet even though she did not feel hungry. Swimming laps in the pool and yoga exercises on the patio in the cool morning relaxed her. She took something to help her sleep. She wrote in a journal about what had happened and how she felt each day. A huge lifesaver was her piano. She had played the piano since sixth grade and was quite accomplished. She could lose herself and all her anxieties in hours of playing Tchaikovsky, Rachmaninoff, Bach, Chopin, Beethoven, Mozart, Debussy, and Liszt.

By May 5, a Tuesday, they all went back to school and work. Tiffany tossed and turned all night not knowing what she would face the first day back. She had to be strong for her family and students. They depended on her. Unknown to her was how deep she would have to dig for the fortitude to survive the weeks ahead.

CHAPTER SEVEN

T HE NIGHT BEFORE RETURNING TO work, Tiffany told her family about her rescue during the riots. They listened in disbelief about the terror she experienced. She still could not place the familiar face in her car window waving her through the intersection.

Tiffany was up early the next morning. Her drive took the longest. Everyone got up as she was leaving. She hugged them all. With a big kiss, she wished them a great day. Bill gave her an extra-long, tender hug and kiss.

Tiffany headed for Leo Politi Elementary School apprehensive about the drive from the freeway to the parking lot. What would be the condition of the neighborhood? Had the rioting run its course? Were all her students going to show up today? What happened to their families these past days? The unknown she faced caused an uneasiness in her stomach. As Tiffany drove through her school's community, all remained calm and quiet. She saw the carnage left from the looting and the fires. Arriving at her classroom, she began the preparations for the day. She heard a knock on her door.

"Good morning," a man greeted her. A Los Angeles School District badge hung around his neck. "I'm George from the maintenance department. We're checking all the schools in riot zones to ensure they're in good condition. A crew has already cleaned up all the ashes on the grounds."

"Everything seems okay," Tiffany responded, "but I have some lights flickering in the back corner."

"I'll be back later to take a look," promised George. "Have a good day."

"Thanks," replied Tiffany, getting back to work.

Soon students and their parents began to arrive. On a normal day, they dropped them off at the gate. Today, they allowed them to bring their children to the classrooms. Tiffany needed to make a secure and safe environment for them at school after their neighborhood trauma.

As Tiffany welcomed each student and parent, they handed her gifts. They expressed their gratefulness and love with flowers and delicious food. The Korean families looked like they bought out the Los Angeles Flower Market that morning. Tiffany lined up the bouquets along the bookcases under the windows. The sea of colors appeared like a bunch of crayons, come alive, decorating the room with happiness.

Other parents brought Tiffany's favorite, homemade tamales. Martin's mom, Kayla, brought perfect fried chicken. Tiffany's classroom had the aroma of a garden restaurant. She eagerly anticipated her lunch break. Their outpouring of appreciation matched her warm-hearted welcomes.

As the parents left for the day, the students settled down, reading at their desks. Marcela appeared at the door. Tiffany hugged her.

"Good morning, Mrs. Carter," greeted a deep voice.

Tiffany looked up at Marcela's dad. She had only seen him at a distance in the pick-up line after school. The startled expression on Tiffany's face showed her astonishment at seeing the face that had appeared outside her car window, waving her to the freeway entrance.

Confounded with surprise she exclaimed, "It was you!"

"Yes, it was me! We found out that you were the last teacher to leave the school so we went out looking for you," he affirmed.

A tear ran down Tiffany's cheek, "How can I ever repay you!"

"Teaching Marcela to read and write is all the payment I need!" he confirmed.

"I appreciate you saving my life!" thanked Tiffany, close to tears.

"My name is Mateo if you ever need help again!" he assured her.

The school day went well. The students were happy to be back. Despite their joy at seeing Tiffany and their friends again, they seemed restless. The atmosphere was filled with tension and they lacked focus. Tiffany pulled out a trick she often used to enhance their concentration. She had been teaching them drumming rhythms on their desks. She used her little Djembe drum to lead them in the intricate patterns. Through her research, she learned that drumming engages both the linear rational left side of the brain and the creative, intuitive right side of the brain. After using drumming to enhance her students' cognitive functions and improve motor skills, Tiffany discovered they also became relaxed. Their concentration improved.

Easing the tension in the classroom, Tiffany's students accomplished some learning. The rest of the day was productive. It was time to walk the students to the gate for parent pick-up. Parents greeted their kids with hugs, holding their hands for the walk home. Martin was the last student left. Tiffany waited for his mom who usually met him.

A young man ran up, "Sorry, I'm late! My mom had a client and couldn't come!"

"This is my brother, Jordan," explained Martin.

"Nice to meet you," said Tiffany.

"You too," Jordan sputtered, grabbing Martin's hand, and spinning around to leave.

An unexplained disquiet spread over Tiffany as she walked back to her classroom. The day went much better than she expected. George returned and replaced her flickering classroom lights. She packed up her gifts and a couple of stunning flower arrangements. It was time to head home. The school staff was required to be out of the buildings by four in the afternoon every day. Due to gang activity, it was not safe to stay for afternoon or evening events. She stepped out into the beautiful day. The warmth caressed her skin. Tiffany looked forward to getting home, seeing her family, and enjoying a dip in the pool.

Jordan rushed Martin home. He bounded upstairs after Martin settled in at his mom's salon desk with a snack and his homework.

"Jasen, I found her!" Jordan burst out.

"Found who?"

"The woman in the car! She's Martin's teacher!" declared Jordan.

"You're joking!" Jasen gasped, incredulous.

CHAPTER EIGHT

O N A BRIGHT AND BEAUTIFUL day at Leo Politi Elementary School, Tiffany and her first-grade class loaded onto a school bus. The enthusiastic children embarked on a memorable field trip to the beach near the Los Angeles International Airport. The air was filled with excitement as the students, accompanied by chaperones and teacher assistants, stepped onto the sandy shores of the Pacific Ocean. The sun painted the sky with hues of blue and white, casting a warm glow over the golden sands. Waves crashed on the shore and scurried up the beach, bringing in tumbled colored rocks and fascinating shells. The children, some of whom had never seen the ocean before, were wide-eyed with wonder.

As the students set foot on the soft sand, they kicked off their shoes and felt the warmth between their tiny toes. A sense of awe glowed on their faces as they discovered seashells scattered along the shoreline. They gathered up the shells, studying the intricate patterns and flashy colors. Laughter and giggles echoed as the boys and girls ran, played, and built sandcastles, displaying their creativity. Tiffany and the chaperones kept a watchful eye, ensuring a safe and enjoyable experience.

Soon Tiffany called everyone over to the picnic tables for lunch. The cafeteria at school packed sack lunches for everyone with sandwiches, fruit, a vegetable pack, cookies, and a drink. The chaperones and assistants passed out the lunches to the hungry group.

Earlier, Tiffany had hurried around the school collecting the lunches, picking up the emergency kit at the office, and securing the parent permission slips. She realized she had left her purse in her desk drawer in all the rush. Normally she locked it in her closet or brought it with her. It was probably safe, she concluded, since her classroom door was locked.

One of the highlights of the field trip was the proximity of the beach to the Los Angeles International Airport, where the children witnessed planes taking off overhead. Every time an airplane roared to life, the kids craned their necks and pointed excitedly, their eyes following the aircraft as it soared into the endless sky.

"Okay, everyone," Tiffany got the students' attention. "We have been learning about countries around the world. We're going to play a game. You have to finish a sentence, telling what country your airplane would fly to and what you would like to do or see there. I'll go first. My airplane would fly me to Costa Rica to climb on hanging bridges in the canopy and fly through the treetops on a zipline. Now it's your turn. Rosa, you go first."

Rosa thought for a minute, "My airplane would fly me to Botswana to go on a safari to see elephants and giraffes."

Kwan spoke, "My airplane would fly me to Australia to see the kangaroos, koalas, crocs, deadly snakes, huge spiders, sharks . . ."

"Okay, that's enough!" interrupted Tiffany, laughing. "Your turn, Aurora."

"My airplane would fly me to Argentina where I would get on a ship to Antarctica to see the Emperor Penguins," she announced.

"Jose, where would your plane fly?" Tiffany asked.

"My airplane would fly me to Egypt to ride a camel to the pyramids," he stated.

And on it went until each student had a turn. Their imaginations were so stimulated that later, they continued choosing countries to fly to among their friends on the bus ride back to school.

After lunch, as the day unfolded, some children braved the gentle waves, dipping their toes into the cool ocean water for the first time. One boy sat at the edge of the waves, letting them swirl around him. Seeing the joy on his face, Tiffany did not worry about his wet clothes. They created lasting memories of a day filled with sunshine, sand, and the boundless wonders of the beach. This field trip became a cherished chapter in the children's early education, leaving them with a newfound appreciation for the world beyond the classroom.

Back at school, Tiffany said goodbye to her class at the gate and got ready to go home. Her purse was safe in her desk drawer. She checked inside. Everything was in its place except her driver's license stuck out of a different pocket. Maybe she put it there without thinking.

Tiffany was weary after a busy, fun-filled day. She walked around the parked cars in the lot toward her car in the far, corner space. Approaching, she noticed an object on the hood of her car. As she got closer, she let out a terrified scream. Another teacher walking to his car heard Tiffany scream and ran to the office for help.

The vice-principal rushed to the parking lot. Tiffany stood frozen on the spot like a statue. All the color had drained from her face. She was trembling. From the hood of her car, a human skull leered out of huge eye cavities. It appeared to be grinning or laughing at her with giant exposed teeth. She felt the evil coldness of death. Rivers, of what looked like blood, ran over the hood from the skull, dripping onto the pavement. Carefully holding Tiffany, the vice-principal led her to the office.

From a dark, deserted classroom across the parking lot, two eyes watched! With a grin of satisfaction, a job well done, he hurried, letting himself out of the service gate.

After the principal's 911 call, the police arrived in minutes. They were shown to Tiffany's car, staring in amazement. Getting to work, they began securing the scene to prevent contamination. Most of the staff had already left for home, so only a few cars remained. The first responding officers placed barrier tape around the perimeter of the parking lot. They needed to control access and preserve the evidence.

The police investigators gathered all the staff still on campus, hoping to identify any potential witnesses. Most would have to be interviewed the next day when they returned to work. The investigators took down everyone's name to be interviewed later. They would need to know each person's relationship to the scene and where they had been during the day.

In the parking lot, documents were written, describing every detail of the scene. The photographer recorded all angles. After they completed their records, the meticulous task of collecting evidence began. Everything was identified, labeled, collected, preserved, packaged, and transported to various laboratories to be analyzed. It was a long, painstaking process.

Tiffany waited in the vice principal's office with an investigator. Bill had been called and was on his way.

"Tiffany," Bill's tight voice greeted her from the doorway. He gathered her in his arms again, holding her close.

The investigator showed Bill to a chair, introducing himself, "My name is Scott, and I will be working on this case."

He described the scene, the skull, and what appeared to be blood running over the hood of the car. Bill looked at him as if he were describing a scene from another planet!

"Either someone climbed the fence or someone from the inside did it," observed Scott. "We are investigating the scene now but it will take a while, so I recommend you both go home tonight."

"When can we have our car?" Bill asked.

"We'll call you when we are finished. At that time, you will be able to take your car home. I would also like to ask Tiffany a few questions before you go," Scott stated.

Scott spoke calmly and gently to Tiffany, "Do you park in that same space every day?"

"Yes," she replied. "I get here early, so I have my choice of spaces."

"Did you see anyone in the parking lot when you arrived?"

"No."

"Do you know of anyone who might want to harm you or traumatize you?"

"No, I can't think of anyone!"

"Were you in your classroom all day?"

"No, I was on a field trip with my students to the beach."

"Was your car locked all day?"

"Yes."

"I need the keys to your car so we can look inside also," Scott requested.

"I have a key you can use," offered Bill.

Tiffany rose, feeling weak, knees shaking. She leaned heavily on Bill as he led her to his car. On their way out, she let the secretary know to get a substitute teacher for her class for the next day.

No one slept well that night at home. The whole bizarre incident made no sense. Tiffany reached for a fluffy fantasy book on her nightstand. She read for most of the dreadful dark hours, trying to escape ghastly nightmares. Despite being tired the next morning, Sidney and Austin went to school. Bill and Tiffany sipped their steaming coffee on the patio in the tranquil coolness. The troubled day dragged by until Scott's call at noon.

"How are you two doing?" Scott inquired.

"Very anxious," replied Bill.

"We completed the initial investigation at the scene. That means we released the car. You can pick it up."

"Do you have any information you can share with us?" asked Bill.

"The red flow lines from the skull appeared to be some kind of paint, not blood," informed Scott.

"That's good news!" Bill said, relieved.

"You'll need to take your car to an auto paint technician," recommended Scott. "I'll keep in touch to let you know our progress."

"Thank you," said Bill.

Bill relayed the conversation to Tiffany.

"Who do you think threatened you?" he asked her.

"The only incident I thought of was my rescue from those three young men who attacked my car."

"Maybe one of them was hurt and wants revenge!" surmised Bill.

"But a death threat! At school!"

"Has anything unusual happened at school since you returned, any little thing?"

Tiffany paused, "I left my purse in my desk drawer when I went on the field trip. When I checked it later, my driver's license and key ring were in a different pocket. That ring had the car key, house key, and the key to my classroom on it."

"We need to let Scott know! We must be alert until they discover who tried to intimidate you!"

An ominous cloud settled over them as they made plans for the next few days, facing a menacing tormentor.

CHAPTER NINE

O VER AT KAYLA'S BEAUTY SALON, she tried to keep up with her usual busy schedule, despite Cameron still being in the hospital. He needed specialized treatment and care for the rest of the month. Most evenings after work, Kayla and Martin caught a city bus to the Good Samaritan Hospital. Jordan's dad would pick them all up for weekend visitations. The visits were heart-wrenching. Counseling would be provided for the family and Cameron to help them cope with such a traumatic situation.

Kayla came down hard on Jordan and Jasen. She made them promise to be in school every day. They had to attend her Baptist church every Sunday. In addition to that, she demanded they both get part-time jobs. Last Sunday, Kayla and the boys went to the morning church service. In light of the carnage caused by the riots, the pastor preached forgiveness. He emphasized God's grace in forgiving every person, no matter what they had done.

"Put forgiveness right at the heart of your world. Believe in love because love and forgiveness are more powerful than cynicism and hate," the pastor instructed. "A certain amount of acceptance (which is not the same as cowardice or indifference) is necessary or you spend your life burning up with annoyance and rage!"

After the church service, Mama fixed their favorite Sunday meal, spicy fried chicken, flavorful collard greens, cornbread, and sweet, juicy peach cobbler for dessert.

While they feasted, Jasen stated, "Mama, I don't think I can forgive those people for what they did to Cameron!"

"Without forgiveness, you will just clutter your life with old business," Kayla responded. "Not forgiving is like scratching a sore to keep the healing scab from forming. It's best to quit scratching. Not forgiving can destroy your life!"

Jordan arrived home the next day with news of a job offer, "Mama, Mr. Kim offered me and Jasen jobs at his market. He needs help with repairs, cleaning, and setting up new shelves. We would be unloading grocery delivery trucks and stocking shelves for a few hours after school every day!"

"Sounds like fine jobs for you two! When do you start?" asked Mama.

"Tomorrow, if that's okay. His store is a mess!"

"I'm proud of you boys!" exclaimed Mama, pleased with their initiative.

Mr. Kim owned the most popular grocery store in the neighborhood. His prices were fair and he stocked cultural foods eaten by the Blacks, Hispanics, and Asian populations in the community. To save his market during the riots, he opened his doors, telling everyone to take anything they wanted. He just asked that they not set the store on fire!

The government provided financial aid and support for the riot-affected communities. Funds were allocated for rebuilding infrastructure, businesses, and homes. Community organizations, non-profits, and religious institutions played a significant role in the rebuilding process. They provided support to individuals and families who had lost their homes or businesses. Efforts were made to encourage businesses to return to the affected areas. This was important for restoring economic stability.

There was damage not only to physical structures but also to community trust. Initiatives focused on fostering dialogue, understanding, and reconciliation. Policy changes, related to law enforcement practices and community-police relations, were addressed. The process aimed not only at physical reconstruction but also visited the root causes of the unrest and promoted lasting positive change.

Kayla's family and her ex-husband, Isaiah's family had been part of the Second Great Migration of the Blacks from Louisiana and other states during the 1940s to the 1970s. Many moved to Los Angeles looking for better jobs and opportunities. Isaiah worked for the Los Angeles School District as a high school gym teacher and a boys' basketball coach. His brother, George, worked in the district's maintenance department. They lived in a remodeled apartment building, sharing a two-bedroom unit.

That evening after work, Isaiah picked up hamburgers for their dinner.

Relaxing in their sunny breakfast nook, George blurted out his news, "I did it! I put the skull on her car with red paint running down the hood!"

"How did it go?" asked Isaiah.

"You should have seen her face! She screamed and froze, white as a sheet! She didn't move until the principal led her away. I watched from an empty classroom, then left through the service gate."

"This is only the beginning! We'll make her suffer for what she did to Cameron! We'll wipe out her whole family!" growled Isaiah, slamming his fist on the table.

CHAPTER TEN

T**IFFANY DROVE TO** L**EO** P**OLITI**, followed by Bill. They decided he would drive behind her every morning to ensure her safety. Arriving at the parking lot gate, he pulled up and got out of his car. She walked over, her reddish-blond hair hung in loose curls, brushing her shoulders. She smiled, her face lighting up, crystal-clear blue eyes sparkling. Tears welled up in Bill's eyes as he watched her approach, memories of happier times fading away.

"You look beautiful," Bill said, gathering her in his arms. "I love you!"

Tiffany kissed him, "I love you, too, handsome!"

"Have a great day!"

Bill headed back to the San Fernando Valley for his work day. He felt comforted knowing Mateo would follow her to the freeway entrance every day after school. He, an uncle, and a few cousins had a small construction company. With a flexible schedule, Mateo could easily slip away.

Tiffany opened her classroom door to find boxes piled in a corner. The pictures on the sides showed Djembe drums. Delighted, she laughed out loud! While Tiffany was applying for teaching positions in the Los Angeles School District, she worked a temporary job for a lubricant manufacturing company. Their products were engineered to help protect and maintain the productivity and efficiency of equipment including automotive, industrial, manufacturing, aerospace, military, and utilities. She processed orders in the office. The owners, a husband and wife, Annabelle, had their offices next door. Tiffany and Annabelle became fast friends. She asked Tiffany what she could do for her classroom. Explaining all the benefits drumming provided for the children's learning and well-being, Annabelle offered to buy a Djembe drum for each student. They had arrived!

Tiffany was so excited that she did not notice George in the doorway.

"Good morning," greeted George. "I stopped by to see if your lights have been working."

"They're working great!" replied Tiffany, slightly startled.

"I also wanted to say how sorry I was to hear about your car the other day!"

"Oh, everything's all right now, thank you!"

"Is there anything you need help with?" offered George.

"Come to think of it, yes! These boxes of Djembe drums need to be unpacked."

George unpacked the boxes while Tiffany arranged the drums along the wall by the corner reading rug. The kids would be ecstatic. She would begin their first lesson today. While Tiffany worked, she explained the benefits of drumming to George.

"I taught with the Peace Corps in Ghana for two years. That's where I learned my Djembe drumming," said Tiffany.

"These kids are sure lucky to have you as a teacher," George commented, noticing her athletic gracefulness and beauty.

She smiled, "I love teaching and want the best for my students!"

"Stay safe!" George expressed as he left with the last of the empty boxes.

"Thank you for your help!"

Tiffany's class worked hard, knowing they would get to drum later in the day. She began with an introduction to the Djembe. It came from West

Africa, originating in Mali. These particular goblet-shaped drums were made in Guinea from a single piece of wood. The bottom, cone-shaped section of the drums, was carved with various African animals, elephants, giraffes, rhinos, lions, and zebras. The head of the drum was covered in goat skin.

It was time to hand out the drums! The students hugged them to their chests, thrilled at the wonderful gift. Tiffany demonstrated how to hold the drum between their knees. The small drums were twelve inches tall with a seven-inch head diameter, the best size for small kids.

Tiffany had already taught them basic drumming techniques on their desks. They reviewed the "slap," "bass," and "tone" sounds. Their faces glowed as the deep, sharp, and mid-pitched sounds resonated throughout the room. Next, Tiffany started with a basic tone rhythm, alternating between the "bass" and the "tone" sounds. The bass was a flat hand bounce in the middle of the drum and the tone was made with the fingers within the two inches at the front edge of the drum. It went Bass (left hand), Tone (right hand), Bass (left), and Tone (right). Once the class had practiced that rhythm, she demonstrated the Heartbeat rhythm which was great for beginners. It went Bass (left), Bass (right), Tone (left), Tone (right). They mastered the rhythms, ready for more complicated patterns.

The rest of the school week proved productive. Jamming all her report-card paperwork in her school bag, Tiffany prepared for the week-end. Her school year was winding down. Her year-round schedule ended at the end of May. She had June off and began a new school year on July 1. She and her class had two months in the classroom and one month off, continuing throughout the year. It was great to have four months off a school year, one month every season. It worked well with her students, taking only a day or two to get back on track after returning.

Mateo followed her to the freeway entrance as promised. Heading home, Tiffany decided she was too weary to cook dinner and picked up her kids' favorite BBQ Chicken pizza and garlic bread. When she got home,

Austin reminded her of his soccer game on Saturday. She looked forward to being in the fresh air, rooting for his team, a report card break.

After the soccer game, which they won in a shoot-out, Sidney and Austin invited friends over for a swim. Tiffany found a quiet spot to work and spread out her report cards. While she reported on each child's progress in first grade, Bill rested. He had a headache in the morning and complained of being tired. She wondered if his headaches were becoming more frequent. Her month off was a week away so she would discuss it with him then.

Tiffany was startled by a crash! She entered the kitchen and saw Bill getting up from the floor.

"Sweetheart, are you okay?" she asked.

"Yes, I tripped on the rug!" he said sharply.

Tiffany tried to concentrate on her schoolwork and soon gave up. The kids got out of the pool and left for a baseball game at their school. She needed a refreshing swim, to relax her muscles and melt the stress away. Bill joined her. They enjoyed a quiet evening alone together.

Tiffany drove back to Leo Politi for her last week of this school year. Bill followed her and gave her a reassuring goodbye hug, the smell of her perfume lingering on his shirt. She fitted her key into her classroom door. It was not locked! She pushed it gently, without stepping in. The hair on the back of her neck rose and her skin began to tingle. She slammed the door shut and dashed to the office. The principal accompanied her back to her room. Cautiously they opened the door, switching on the lights. Djembe drums were scattered on the floor like bowling pins after a strike.

Picking one up, Tiffany cried out, "The goat skin head has been slashed!"

The principal grabbed another drum, "This one has been cut too! How could this happen!"

Checking each drum, they all were cut open. It was devastating!

"I don't know!" Tiffany sank into her chair.

The principal and Tiffany decided to put the drums in a storage closet. She told her students that they needed to be repaired. Whoever slashed the drums knew how important they were to her. The skull and the drums were psychological warfare! She spent an anxious week determined to survive until her well-needed break.

Tiffany prepared a special presentation, honoring each student for his year's achievements. It was a sad goodbye but she would see them again in July for second grade. Her program included first and second grades with the same class, keeping consistency.

Mateo waited at the gate to follow Tiffany through the dangerous city blocks. She thanked him, firmly shaking his hand and expressing her gratitude. They drove to the freeway not paying any attention to a Los Angeles School District maintenance van following them. Arriving at the freeway, it continued to follow Mateo to his job site.

CHAPTER ELEVEN

TIFFANY WAS HOME FOR HER vacation from school. She felt upbeat. Austin and Sidney had two more weeks before their school year ended. She spent the first week catching up on friendships and calls to her parents and Bill's parents.

Tiffany met her friend, Annabelle, for an early dinner at the Bonaventure Hotel's revolving Lounge and Restaurant. She insisted on treating Tiffany to a luxurious culinary delight. She stepped into the hotel lobby where the sunlight refracted through prisms on beveled glass door edges, casting rainbows throughout. As it poured down through skylights, it reflected off artificial ponds and through Bamboo gardens, creating rippling and shafted light patterns on the walls. Annabelle met her in the lobby. They zipped up the glass-enclosed elevator to the thirty-fourth floor. The Lounge boasted soaring views of Downtown Los Angeles as it revolved. Annabelle ordered a Chilled Seafood Platter for two and Lychee Martinis to sip. As they enjoyed the ever-changing panoramic views, the lights of the city sparkled like a field of diamonds. They completed their seafood delights with perfect pan-seared salmon. It had a beautiful, deliciously seasoned golden crust and a barely cooked center. The side dishes were savory Cauliflower Puree with thyme and French Green Beans with shallots. Accompanying the meal was a white wine, Sauvignon Blanc, coupled with a crisp dryness and light body to compliment the flavorful salmon.

Annabelle and Tiffany relaxed and shared what was happening in their lives. She relayed the sad story of the Djembe drums. Annabelle would inquire at the company where she purchased them to see if they could be repaired. It was a shocking story. She was more concerned about Tiffany's safety. Back down in the lobby as they parted, Annabelle kissed Tiffany on the cheek, wishing her friend rest and rejuvenation on her break from school.

The next day, Tiffany called her parents who lived in a suburb north of Seattle. She tried to keep the conversation mostly about how they were doing and news about the kids. She and her mom, Elizabeth, were very close. When she was in Junior High School, her dad had died of cancer, leaving them brokenhearted with grief. They supported each other through the following years. Her mom met a widower, Chase, at work where he served as the Chaplin in a senior community and she was the Activities Director. At first, Tiffany was resentful of having to share her mom's attention. Her mom and Chase were married and he turned out to be a thoughtful and kind man, never making her feel left out. Tiffany appreciated his love and care for her mom. She and Bill looked forward to her parents' visit for a week at Christmas.

Tiffany caught up on spring cleaning around the house. Since she had extra time, she decided to surprise Bill with his favorite meal. Austin and Sidney were going to an end-of-the-year party with friends in the evening. She and Bill would have a romantic evening alone together. Tiffany prepared Chicken and Prosciutto Cordon Bleu. She pounded the chicken cutlets until they were a quarter inch thick, seasoning them all over with salt and pepper. Then, she arranged prosciutto and Swiss cheese on the bottom halves of the cutlets. Starting at the bottom, she tightly rolled up the chicken. Next, she brushed the stuffed chicken all over with sour cream. She pressed them into the panko mixture, coating all sides. To make the mixture, she roasted the panko in butter until it was golden and fragrant. Putting it in a shallow dish, she stirred in garlic powder, chopped parsley, and a pinch each of salt and pepper. With the seams down on a baking sheet, she roasted the chicken on the top rack at 425 degrees for 20 minutes. While the chicken was cooked, she made the sauce to go on it. Tiffany softened chopped shallots in a drizzle of oil with a pinch of salt. Then, she stirred in water and chicken stock concentrate. When the liquid had reduced by half, she removed the pan from the heat, stirring in mustard, garlic herb butter, and sour cream. To compliment the meal, she made Herbed Vegetable Rice Pilaf.

After the kids had left for their party, Tiffany served Bill on the patio surrounded by their luscious gardens. A candle flickered on the table between them, lighting Bill's rugged features, sandy brown hair, and piercing blue eyes. He poured the delicious Burgundy Chardonnay into their wine glasses. They toasted vacation and their enduring love for each other.

"This is magnificent," Bill complimented, tasting his chicken smothered in sauce. "Thank you!"

"I don't get to spoil you very often!" Tiffany beamed.

After dinner, they sipped their wine. Bill put on dreamy music, and love songs from the '80s. The full moon hung low in the sky, casting a soft, silver glow over the yard. The picturesque sky was so clear, that you could almost see every crater.

Tiffany felt a tap on her shoulder, "May I have this dance?" a deep voice asked.

Looking up with a dazzling smile, she rose, folding into Bill's waiting arms. Millions of stars were sprinkled around them as they swayed to the music. A couple of times Bill stepped on Tiffany's toes. She never said a word, lost in the romance of the evening.

The sun streamed through the bedroom window. Tiffany realized she had slept in. It was Saturday. Austin and Sidney left early to play a few games of tennis with friends. Later in the afternoon, they would cheer for Austin's soccer team.

Sidney had driven home from the park and Austin was riding his bicycle home. He loved riding and rode around the neighborhood most days after school.

"Did you see Austin when you drove home?" Tiffany asked Sidney.

"No, he must have gone a different route," she answered.

"You would think he'd be home by now!" observed Bill.

"Do you want me to look for him?" offered Sydney.

"No, I'm sure he'll be back any minute."

Bill heard the doorbell. Before he could get there, Tiffany opened the door. Two police officers were standing on the porch.

"May I help you?" she asked.

"Are you Mr. and Mrs. Carter?" one of the officers inquired.

"Yes," said Bill.

"Do you have a son named, Austin?"

"Yes, why?"

"He has been in a bicycle accident. The aid car took him to the Northridge Hospital on Roscoe Boulevard." informed the officer. "We found his Student Identification Card in his wallet."

"Is he badly hurt?" questioned Tiffany, with a catch in her voice.

"He was unconscious. We recommend you meet him at the hospital emergency room! We are investigating the accident scene and will share any information we gather as soon as possible."

Stunned, no one said a word! Tiffany, Bill, and Sidney grabbed what they needed and ran to the car. A heavy silence threatened to crush them as they drove to the emergency room.

CHAPTER TWELVE

The DAY FINALLY CAME WHEN Cameron was released from the hospital. Kayla put up a "Welcome Home" sign across the living room wall. BBQ ribs were slow-cooking in the oven, filling the apartment with a mouthwatering aroma. A sweet potato pie sat on a cooling rack on the kitchen counter.

As Cameron walked through the back door, tears filled his eyes, "I didn't know if I would ever get back home again!"

Jordan and Jasen took the day off from working at the market to spend time with their family. After Isaiah dropped Cameron off, they sat around the kitchen table, eating ribs slathered in a tangy barbecue sauce. Martin bubbled over with excitement and couldn't stop talking. Kayla sat back, so ecstatic to have her boy back home! Their laughter warmed her heart. Cameron got an extra-large slice of pie!

Cameron had been receiving physical therapy, which would continue. Emotional support and counseling were provided for him as well as their family. They would care for him until he was ready to go back to school. The most important part of his healing was the love and support he had from his family, friends, and their church. Kayla and Martin had been helping to organize food and clothing donations at the church. Many riot victims needed help until they could get back on their feet. She planned on taking

Cameron with them to volunteer. He would need something meaningful to do during his recovery.

Driving home to his apartment, Isaiah seethed inside. Cameron still had a challenging road ahead of him. It was not fair. Those responsible needed to be punished. It was time to step up the pain.

"George," he called when he opened the apartment door. "Would you like to go for a drive? I want to check out where that teacher lives and the neighborhood. We need to make some serious plans!"

"Maybe we've done enough," responded George.

"You didn't see Cameron! He won't ever be the same again!"

"Okay, I've got the address."

Isaiah and George had grown up with their grandparents. Their parents were killed in a car accident when Isaiah was nine years old and George was eight years old. Their grandparents did the best they could to raise them. It was difficult to make ends meet. They seemed to be always working. Despite their demanding jobs, they did make time to take the boys fishing and picnicking by the river in the park. They also attended as many sports competitions as they could fit into their busy schedules. Isaiah was a great three-point shooter in basketball. George played first base in baseball. He could hit the ball out of the park. He got along well with them but Isaiah had a difficult time accepting their love in place of his parents' love. He was hurt, angry, and rebellious.

The boys' grandfather encouraged them to join the army. As soon as they were seventeen and eighteen years old, they signed up to become enlisted soldiers. After their two-year terms, they took advantage of their GI Bills. Isaiah went into education becoming a gym teacher and basketball coach. George was interested in the trades, learning general repairs and maintenance from electrical to plumbing. They balanced each other's personalities with Isaiah's angry spirit and mellow George, trying to keep things on an even keel.

Isaiah and George drove to Northridge in the San Fernando Valley. After locating Tiffany's house, they parked down the block and watched. Soon, a car pulled into the driveway, and teenagers, a girl and a boy, got out and went inside. Another car arrived and parked next to it. A man with a briefcase joined them inside.

"That must be the dad and the two kids coming home from work and school," George observed.

"Tomorrow is Saturday," said Isaiah. "I want to be here early and see what they do on the weekends."

The next morning George and Isaiah were in the neighborhood early, parked in a different location so as not to draw any attention. They saw Sidney and Austin come out of the house with tennis rackets. They threw them into the back seat of the car. Sidney drove off but Austin opened the garage door and brought out a bicycle.

George and Isaiah followed them at a distance to the neighborhood park a few blocks away. They parked in the lot, watching them play tennis with a couple of other kids. After they had played a set, they went their separate ways. Sidney drove home and Austin rode his bicycle.

With Isaiah driving, he and George followed Austin. George heard the car accelerate. Austin looked back, hearing the "vroom" of a car speeding up behind him. He could hear the motor racing! The solid line of parked cars at the curb built a barrier he could not get around until the end of the block. He raced toward his chance of escape! Austin took big breaths like he was having trouble getting enough air! His muscles tensed! His hands were sweaty and slippery on the handlebars! Fear gripped his heart as it pounded in his chest!

"Don't hit him!" George yelled. "You'll kill him!"

There was a sickening thud as the car hit the back of the bicycle! It crunched under the wheels of the car as Isaiah sped down the block like a wild man! Austin flew into the air like a stuntman shot out of a cannon. He sailed over a parked car and crumpled to the ground. His inert form lay unconscious enshrouded in a world of darkness.

CHAPTER THIRTEEN

Bill and Tiffany signed in at the Northridge Hospital's accident and emergency department.

The nurse told them to wait. "I'll let the doctor know you are here," she said.

Excruciating minutes went by. The doctor and the nurse walked out to greet them.

"I'm Dr. Clark," he introduced himself. "We have Austin stabilized but he is still unconscious, as a result of a head injury. He is being prepared for a CT (Computerized Tomography) scan. That will let us know if he has any skull fractures, evidence of bleeding in the brain, blood clots, bruised brain tissue, or swelling. He may also have some fractured ribs and a broken leg. The Radiology team will X-ray for those later."

"Can we see him?" asked Bill.

"Yes," responded Dr. Clark. "You can see him before we begin the CT scan."

Tiffany, Bill, and Sidney walked tentatively into the room. Austin was being given oxygen and had an IV inserted in his arm. Machines were monitoring his vital signs.

Tiffany took his limp hand in hers, daring to look at his deathly pale face. "We're here with you, Austin. We love you. We'll talk to you soon when you wake up," she said with confidence.

Tiffany and her family sat huddled together in the cold, sterile waiting room of the hospital, their faces etched with worry and fear. The air was thick with tension as they anxiously awaited news about their precious son, Austin. They still knew nothing about what was involved in the harrowing bicycle accident.

Bill, a normally stoic man with a kind smile, was now nervously tapping his fingers against the armrest of his chair. His eyes were fixed on the door leading to the doctor's office, desperately seeking any sign of an update. Tiffany, her usually cheerful demeanor replaced with a pained expression, held onto a crumpled tissue in her hands. She occasionally glanced at Bill, silently conveying the shared burden of their anxiety.

Sidney sat quietly with her parents, her wide eyes filled with confusion and concern. She struggled to comprehend the gravity of the situation. The palpable tension in the room told her that this could be life-changing for Austin.

As they waited, the family exchanged glances, trying to offer silent reassurances to one another. Yet, the uncertainty of Austin's condition weighed heavily on their hearts. The room, usually a hub of bustling medical activity, now seemed eerily quiet, amplifying their sense of isolation in this moment of crisis. Amid the stark white walls and harsh fluorescent lighting, Tiffany prayed that the doctor would bring news of Austin's stable condition.

The quiet hallway came alive with hurried footsteps. They looked up to see Dr. Clark approaching.

"Hello," he greeted them. "Sorry for the long wait! We wanted to get all the X-rays done. Austin is waking up. He's asking for you."

"How is he doing?" asked Bill.

"He's stable. The radiologist will read the X-rays and send the results to me. I'll let you know as soon as they arrive. Right now, Austin's body and brain need to have maximum rest. We don't know yet the extent of his brain injury."

"Thank you," said Tiffany.

Dr. Clark led them back to the room and checked Austin again. "Your family is here, Austin. I'll be back soon."

They gathered around his broken body. Tiffany gently kissed him on the cheek. Bill enclosed Austin's clammy hand protectively between his large hands. Sidney lightly stroked his arm.

"We're glad you're awake," Sidney struggled.

"What happened?" he asked groggily.

"We don't know yet," responded Tiffany.

"You had an accident on your bike. You are getting good care here at the Northridge Hospital. You'll be fine and home soon!" assured Bill in a strong voice.

Austin was silent as if trying to recall what had happened to him. "I don't remember," he whispered.

At that moment a nurse walked in to check Austin's vital signs. "How are you feeling?"

"My head hurts," he winced.

"I'll give you something to help relieve that," she reassured, adjusting his IV.

Austin shut his eyes. Soon he was asleep, resting, shutting out the confusing world around him.

There was a soft knock. A nurse stepped into the room.

"The police investigating Austin's accident are here. They would like to talk with you. There's a room down the hallway where you can meet," she said.

As they sat with the policemen around a conference table, Tiffany felt ill. Dread filled her whole being. Did she have the courage and strength to face what she suspected?

The men introduced themselves as Sergeant Jim and Sergeant Rodrigo. They expressed their deep sympathy for Austin's condition.

"We have been assessing the scene of your son's bicycle accident. The scene has been documented and we have collected the evidence. Some witnesses have been interviewed," introduced Rodrigo. "Jim will report what we know so far."

Jim began, "Austin was riding his bicycle north in the 600 block of Palm Drive. A family heard the roar of a car engine and looked out of their front window. A car was racing down the street. It slammed into the back of the bicycle. Austin flew over a car parked beside the curb. He landed on the sidewalk on the other side. The racing car sped on, running over the bicycle. By the time they had run outside, the car had disappeared around the next corner. Seeing Austin was not moving, they called 911. We have taken the bicycle in to analyze it in case there is evidence that would help us identify the car. That is all we know for now. We are knocking on doors down the block, and identifying other potential witnesses. Do you have any questions?"

The Carter family sat motionless, astonished, and bewildered. The news overwhelmed them with shock!

"Did the car accidentally run into Austin's bicycle?" inquired Bill in denial.

"We don't think so," replied Jim. "Witnesses saw the car deliberately target him. There were no skid marks, so it didn't try to slow down or avoid him."

"How could anyone do such a horrific thing!" Sidney exclaimed, her eyes flashing.

"We are always asking ourselves that same question," Jim gently responded.

"We wanted to give you the initial report," informed Rodrigo. "We will keep you updated. Meanwhile, take care of your son. We wish him the very best outcome!"

"Thank you," said Bill.

They slowly made their way back to Austin's room. Fear gripped them as they puzzled over who would want to harm Austin. Tiffany came to the terrifying realization that this was a turning point. Her family was in danger! The threat had escalated, creating an ominous urgency!

CHAPTER FOURTEEN

T HE ATMOSPHERE IN AUSTIN'S ROOM at the Northridge Hospital was heavy with anxiety and sorrow. Tiffany, Bill, and Sidney gathered around his bed, each grappling with the uncertainty of his recovery.

Bill was engulfed with a mix of anger and concern. He struggled to comprehend the senseless act that led to his son's injuries. His face reflected a blend of frustration and helplessness. The reality was that someone intentionally tried to harm Austin.

Tiffany sat by his bedside, visibly distraught, fighting to hold back the tears. She clutched Austin's hand, offering silent support and comfort. The pain etched on her face revealed the depth of her maternal anguish, compounded by the shock of the hit-and-run accident.

Sidney stayed strong for her family, torn between fear and responsibility. Her protective instincts kicked in as she processed the deliberate attack on her younger brother. She put on a brave front, hiding her distress. Her parents and, more importantly, her injured brother needed her support.

The hospital room became a space where grief, anger, and disbelief intermingled. Medical equipment beeped, constantly reminding them of the severity of the situation. They whispered conversations and exchanged worried glances. Their shared vulnerability united them as they considered how to navigate the difficult journey ahead. Tiffany knew they were resilient. They would take one step at a time!

A nurse entered the room to check on Austin. She invited them to meet the doctor in the same conference room where they met the police.

Dr. Clark warmly greeted them, "I have the results of all the X-rays. He has mild brain trauma. I would like to keep Austin here for observation for a couple of days, watching for further symptoms. Some of them could be headaches, nausea, vertigo, memory loss, sensory overload, and visual problems. Recovery time will be three to six months. Our healthcare team will meet with you to give you instructions for homecare."

"Does he have broken ribs?" Tiffany asked.

"Yes, he has two fractured ribs and a broken tibia. The ribs will take about six weeks to heal. The broken leg will heal in three to six months."

"He has a long road ahead of him!" observed Bill.

"Tomorrow morning at 10:00, the healthcare team will meet you here. They will give you directions on how to prepare for Austin's homecoming."

No one in the family would go home that night and leave Austin. Mom stretched out on the firm couch under the window. Dad dozed off in a reclining chair. Sidney curled up on the foot of his bed in case he woke up and needed anything. They were watchful and alert.

After meeting with the healthcare team in the morning, the family split up to get their part of the preparations completed. Bill headed to his work office at the Northeast Health Corporation where he had access to a wheelchair they could borrow. Tiffany went to the pharmacy to pick up a long list of medications. Sidney stayed home to prepare Austin's room. She moved obstacles and arranged his bedroom to make it accessible and comfortable. She put a bedside table on each side of his bed so whatever he needed would be within arm's reach. She removed potential hazards around the house to prevent accidents or falls and ensured pathways were clear. It was reassuring to anticipate Austin's return home.

The family rendezvoused after completing their tasks.

"Before going back to the hospital, I want to see where the accident happened," suggested Bill.

Finding the location, they walked around and imagined the terrifying events. A lady came out of the house where Austin had landed.

"Are you the boy's family?" she asked.

"Yes, it was our son, Austin, who was hit by the car," Bill replied.

The lady told them the awful story. They thanked her for calling 911 and sharing what they heard and saw with the police.

They walked down the block, feeling Austin's panic. A man stepped out of his house and approached them.

"Hello," he greeted them, "I'm Neville. I heard the roar of the car when your son's bicycle was hit by the car. I'm a retired detective and have been following this case out of sheer curiosity."

"Nice to meet you. I'm Bill. Have you learned anything yet?" Bill inquired.

"No, but I would like to talk to you about allowing me to investigate alongside the law enforcement agencies. I'm an expert at solving crimes in my unorthodox way!"

"We would certainly consider that," acknowledged Bill. "We'll contact you after we get our son home and settled."

"Thank you," Neville handed them a business card. "I do have some immediate advice," he continued. "I would call a home security company for an appointment as soon as possible to install a security system. Meanwhile, I could recommend a security guard until it gets installed."

They looked at him in shock!

After a brief hesitation, Tiffany spoke, "We hadn't gotten that far in our thinking yet. We've just been focused on taking care of Austin!"

"I understand," empathized Neville. "Whoever hit your son knows where you live. If they are out to harm your family, they will be back! I have a friend I used to work with on the police force. He has a private security guard company. I could get a guard out to your home within an hour. That would give you peace of mind, bringing Austin home. You could focus on him and not worry about your family's safety."

"Thank you," Bill made a decision. "We would appreciate you doing that. We can meet with you tomorrow."

Returning to the hospital, everyone felt a slight burden lifted. Austin was more alert. They shared with him the plan and preparations for his homecoming the next day.

"I guess I won't be playing soccer for a while," he realized.

"You'll be back stronger than ever," encouraged Sidney, squeezing his arm.

"You need some healing. We're all here to help you!" exclaimed Tiffany. "Your soccer team can't wait until the doctor says they can visit you!"

A grin spread across Austin's face. The first one they had seen in days!

Austin was released from the hospital into the family's care the next day. Tiffany lined up his medications. She recorded them, dosages, and timings in a notebook. In another section, she wrote in the appointments scheduled for follow-up. She wrote a list of emergency contacts, including healthcare professionals, neighbors, and relatives. Another part had emergency procedures in case of unexpected situations. Combining medical care, family support, and a well-organized home environment, this plan aimed to facilitate a smooth and effective recovery for Austin.

Sidney was in charge of his deep breathing exercises to prevent complications like pneumonia. She recorded each exercise session in the notebook. Bill was in charge of keeping an eye out for any signs of complications, such as changes in mental status, difficulty breathing, or increased pain. Tiffany took responsibility for administering the medications and providing nutritious meals.

When they arrived home with Austin, the security guard was at the front of the house as Neville had promised. He introduced himself and continued his duties, assuring them of his protection. They could see him walking around the perimeter of the yard at regular intervals.

The next day, Bill had arranged to meet with Neville to form a game plan for their security and a plan of action to investigate the hit-and-run accident. The unresolved tensions of unanswered questions jeopardized the well-being and future of their family. Menacing clouds darkened their lives. They felt an acute awareness of malicious and sinister danger. It threatened them with the fear of impending disaster.

CHAPTER FIFTEEN

L EAVING SIDNEY IN CHARGE OF Austin's care at home, Bill and Tiffany stepped outside into their front yard. The security guard was coming around the corner.

"Good morning," he smiled.

"Good morning," Bill responded. "By the way, I made an appointment to have the security system installed next week. I hope you can stay."

"Of course, I'll be here as long as you need me! Another guard will "spell me" so I can get some sleep. I'll be back for the night shift."

"Thank you! Please let us know if there is anything you need."

Bill took Tiffany's hand as they walked down the sidewalk to Neville's home. A pleasant breeze showered them with the flower petals off the Jacaranda trees. Purple rain fell on the sidewalk like a flower girl spreading petals down the aisle at a wedding ceremony. Beautiful blossoms painted the sky every year in April and May. Their mild fragrance was fading, the delicate blooms giving way to bright green, feathery, fern-like leaves.

When they reached Neville's home, he invited them to his comfortable seating area on his patio. He served a sweet lemonade to cool them after their walk. Neville left the police force after a distinguished career, but his passion for justice and solving mysteries persisted. Whether offering guidance to the new generation of detectives or solving cold cases for his satisfaction, he remained skilled at connecting seemingly unrelated dots.

"Tiffany," Neville began, "I need you to tell me every detail of events from your attack during the riots until the bicycle accident."

She relayed the frightening story, pausing now and then to steady her quavering voice. Bill touched her arm reassuringly. When she was done, Neville sat in silence. Only the murmuring of the Palm leaves overhead disturbed the quiet.

"I have a plan," he spoke up. "If you will allow me to investigate, I'll begin gathering information on these cases. I would like to spend the first week you return to school following you around. I need to see, hear, and feel the environment and meet the people you work with. Maybe I can start finding some answers. Meanwhile, only go out when you need to and never be alone!"

"That sounds like a great plan! Would that work for you, Sweetheart?" Bill looked at Tiffany.

"Yes, I'll make sure my principal is informed and get his approval."

Later that evening, relaxing in the late-night air by the pool, Bill and Tiffany had a chance to talk.

"Austin did well today," Tiffany sighed with relief. "How did you think it went?"

Bill hesitated, "Very well. I'm afraid as the days drag on in recovery, he may become depressed."

"We'll keep on top of that. As soon as we get the doctor's approval, I'd like to invite his friends to come over."

"That would cheer him up!"

"I've been thinking," mused Tiffany. "I go back to school soon. We need help taking care of Austin. They want you back at your office. Sidney has a volleyball camp that I don't want her to miss."

"What do you suggest?"

"I was wondering if your mom would come down for July and my mom for August. Your mom is a nurse, so she would be beneficial for the initial weeks. We have the guestroom suite next to the family room. They would be very comfortable and private. Then, I will be home again for my break in September."

"That would relieve a lot of pressure," agreed Bill. "Let's call them tomorrow."

"Bill," she looked at him fondly, "I haven't forgotten about your headaches. Are you still having them?"

"They're not too bad. I think it's stress from the riots and all that has happened since."

"Well, if they get any worse, please let me know."

Time flew by. Tiffany prepared for her new school year. She was in a Masters'/Doctorate program at California State Northridge. Her project for her degree entailed teaching her students reading and writing in Spanish and English simultaneously. At present, the Los Angeles School District taught the Spanish-speaking students only how to read and write in Spanish. They had to show proficiency in Spanish before they received English instruction. Many did not pass the testing until fourth grade. She felt that placed the students far behind, making it difficult for them to comprehend the higher-level academic subjects. Many students dropped out of high school before graduation.

Tiffany's project involved a bilingual approach, splitting the school day between English and Spanish instruction. She had a partner teacher who taught her class in Spanish for half of the day. Then they traded students. Tiffany taught her partner's class in English while she was teaching Tiffany's class in Spanish. She kept the Korean students all day, immersing them in English. The students would be tested every year, recording their progress. The program would follow their success for four years.

Tiffany's premise was that a bilingual educational approach offered benefits for Spanish-speaking students. It allowed the Spanish students to maintain and strengthen proficiency in their native language. It preserved their cultural identity and fostered a deeper connection to their heritage. For part of the day, immersion in an English-speaking environment accelerated language acquisition, aiding in fluency and comprehension. Implementing a program in both languages offered students a comprehensive and enriched educational experience that supported their linguistic, cognitive, academic, and socio-cultural development.

Bilingual education improved the students' cognitive abilities. They included skills such as better problem-solving, multitasking abilities, and higher levels of creativity. Learning in both languages promoted cultural awareness and understanding, fostering empathy and a broader worldview.

Bilingual education correlated with better academic performance across subjects. Students comprehended complex concepts in both languages, leading to higher achievement levels. Being proficient in two languages provided students with adaptability skills, enabling them to navigate diverse environments and collaborate effectively in multicultural settings.

In addition to those benefits, Bilingual education fostered an inclusive environment, allowing students from diverse linguistic backgrounds to feel valued and included in the school community. It enabled better communications between students, their families, and educators, facilitating stronger connections and involvement in the student's education.

Tiffany felt the pressure bearing down on her, preparing for school and caring for Austin. She established a daily routine, giving her a sense of stability and predictability. Early in the morning after kissing Bill goodbye as he left for work, she meditated and relaxed with yoga exercises. She fixed a healthy breakfast for Sidney and Austin. Then, she worked on planning for the upcoming school year. Annabelle came over for a few visits, providing her friend, Tiffany, emotional validation and understanding. After a nutritious lunch, she engrossed herself in her piano music, playing as if she were performing on a stage accompanied by an orchestra. If she had time, she would bring out her Djembe drum, practicing complicated rhythms. Every night, after a delicious, healthful meal with her family, they wheeled

Austin out to the patio. They talked about their day and planned for the future. Tiffany's day would not be complete without swimming laps in the pool and soaking in the hot tub with Bill. As night settled in, she thought about how the terrifying events since the riots were impacting her family. Her breath quickened. A shiver ran down her spine. She felt a dark, perilous cloud hanging over her head.

CHAPTER SIXTEEN

School at Leo Politi Elementary would be back in session for Tiffany in a couple of days. Everything was being organized at home for Austin's care. Bill's mom, Shirley, had flown into the Burbank airport the night before. She was settling into her suite and studying everyone's schedule and the requirements for Austin's routine. Her nursing specialty was neuro-oncology at the University of Washington Medical Center in Seattle, Washington, treating brain tumors and other tumors of the nervous system. Austin was in excellent hands! Tiffany and Bill felt relieved to have her professional supervision, mitigating some of their stress. Even more comforting was Austin having the loving attentiveness of a grandma!

That evening, their family celebrated Shirley's stay with dinner on the welcoming patio. Sidney pushed Austin's wheelchair up to the table. This was the bright spot of his day. It highlighted the positive impact of Tiffany's routines on her family. Their conversations were filled with laughter and love, creating a warm and joyful atmosphere. Moments, like this, strengthened their bond. They gave them hope for the future.

Neville joined Tiffany on the first day of her new school year. Excitement built up inside her as she looked forward to seeing her students again. They loved her. She inspired them to work hard and do their best.

Tiffany had the same class she had for second grade that she had for first grade, ensuring their solid foundation in the basics of reading and math. The most important desire she wanted to leave with them was a love for learning.

On the first day of school, parents were allowed to deliver their child to his classroom. The Korean parents showered Tiffany with gifts of gorgeous flower arrangements. One family brought an elegant indoor Chinese Elm Bonsai tree. The Spanish-speaking families brought her favorite dishes, taco fillings, Machaca burritos, Pozole de Pollo (chicken stew), Cochinita Pibil (pork stew), tamales, enchiladas, Mole, and Tlayuda (Mexican pizza). She had enough food to feed her family for a week! This was their way of showing her their deep appreciation.

It was a delightful scene as Neville took it all in, never having seen anything like it. He met the parents and made a special note to introduce himself to Mateo. The warmth and friendship Tiffany exuded created a joyous reunion for everyone.

Neville obtained a class list from Tiffany with the names of the students and parents. Throughout the week, he noted people who came and went during the school day, signing in at the office. He got a list of the staff from the principal and made time to meet them all. Neville followed her students to music, gym, and computer classes, getting the input and information he needed. He observed everyone's interactions with Tiffany with his keen sense of perception. He never missed a detail.

At the end of the school day, Tiffany was gathering her work to take home. A head popped in the door.

"Hello, Mrs. Carter."

Tiffany looked up, "Oh, hello, George."

"How was your month off?"

"Well, my son was in a bicycle accident so my time was spent taking care of him."

"So sorry to hear that! Is he okay?"

"Yes, he is resting and we are watching him for any signs of complications. George, I'd like you to meet, Neville, a friend of our family, who has been assisting me this week," introduced Tiffany.

George took in Neville's tanned, well-maintained physique and piercing eyes. The intensity of his stare felt like it could penetrate right into George's mind and thoughts.

Neville firmly shook his hand, "Nice to meet you, George."

"George is our maintenance man and fixed problems I was having with my classroom lights," explained Tiffany.

"You probably know the answer to this, George. Do you know who has a key for access to this classroom?" asked Neville.

"It would only be Tiffany, the principal, the custodian, and myself."

"Is there any possibility of putting a deadbolt on the door? Maybe only the custodian would have a key to let people into the room. That would also ensure Tiffany was accompanied when she comes in the early mornings."

"I could handle that," assured George. "I'll need to submit a work order and wait for approval. That's a great idea!"

"Thank you!" said Tiffany.

George remarked about work he needed to get done and hurried from the room. Those probing eyes made him feel uncomfortable. When he left today, he would check the "sign in" list at the office for Neville's last name. An uneasy, forbidding feeling crept over him, sensing an underlying threat. He needed to find out who this "friend of our family" really was.

Arriving home, Tiffany found that everything was running smoothly. She settled down to prepare for the next day's lessons. The reading instruction program she taught was based on scientific research done at Harvard University. She had studied with an expert who had taught thousands of students around the world to read using this method. The program scientifically cooperated with the whole brain by streamlining the flow of incoming data, which simplified and accelerated the process of learning to read. The method taught reading skills in small, simple, step-by-step increments. Each step reinforced the previous steps so students gradually developed reading proficiency.

As students' reading skills improved, their self-confidence and self-esteem also improved. They began making noticeable improvements in other academic areas as well, helping to ensure their success in school and their futures. This reading instruction program made learning to read what it should be: fast, fun, and easy.

The first lesson in Tiffany's reading course taught the five short vowels and the sixteen consonants that have only one sound. After this lesson, non-readers could already read three hundred words! That was powerful. Instead of trying to memorize over one million words in English, students were empowered to read thousands and thousands of words. She prepared her class for reading with a solid foundation. Then she built on that foundation with more and more complex phonics tools until they were reading fluently at an independent level. They each left with his notebook which contained all the rules and instructions needed to refresh or relearn any of the reading information. It would serve them throughout all of their years. It was Tiffany's gift to them!

Having Shirley's help at home gave Tiffany some time to herself. She treasured the time to take inventory of the whirlwind of emotions she had experienced as she navigated the unsettling events unfolding around her. She leaned back in the soothing hot tub, relaxing her muscles. Neville's presence at her school added an element of both anxiety and hope for her. On one hand, she was anxious about the seriousness of the situation as he delved into the past attack during the Rodney King riots and the recent disturbing incidents involving her and her family. On the other hand, there was a glimmer of hope that Neville might uncover crucial information and provide a sense of security.

The bleeding skull left on the hood of Tiffany's car left her feeling targeted and violated. The symbolism of the slashed heads of her classroom

Djembe drums added a personal touch to the attacks, impacting her professional space. She experienced a mix of anger, frustration, and vulnerability.

The hit-and-run accident involving Austin added an intense layer of fear and concern for Tiffany's family's safety. It was such a traumatic incident, evoking a deep sense of helplessness and anguish. She was grappling with guilt and the weight of responsibility for Austin's well-being.

Tiffany was determined to fortify her immediate surroundings. The security system was installed at home. Neville's idea of a deadbolt in her classroom door gave her a feeling of some control. She was at the point of desperation for answers and a resolution.

CHAPTER SEVENTEEN

IT WAS A SAVORED OCCASION at Kayla's cozy home on Sunday afternoon. The fragrant smell of their mom's Southern Fried Chicken had drawn the family around the kitchen table. Her boys relaxed, laughing and talking. While they attended church, the chicken was marinated in buttermilk to tenderize it. She dredged the chicken in spicy, seasoned flour, giving it a crispy-crunchy coating. Then she fried the pieces in peanut oil in the old cast-iron skillet. Buttermilk biscuits were baking in the oven. The tangy-flavored coleslaw was chilling. It was a warm and delightful atmosphere, catching up on everyone's week.

While she cared for Cameron, Kayla had cut back on her clientele at the beauty salon. He started attending his ninth-grade classes at the high school. She was back to busy, full days.

"Mom, my gym class has been running on the track this past week. I like it. I'm pretty fast. Would it be okay if I turned out for track and field? The coach said I could try the running events and maybe some jumping." Cameron wondered what his mom thought.

"That sounds like a great idea. You could try it and see how it works for you." Kayla approved.

"The counselor suggested I might like to get involved in an activity at school. Running made me feel free, calm, and relaxed."

"I think running would be helpful in your healing and recovery from your burns." Kayla reasoned. "When would you start?"

"Tomorrow I can turn out after school. Dad said he could drive me home some days so I don't have to wait for a bus."

"Sounds like you have a good plan!" Kayla encouraged him, realizing his involvement in track and field could play a pivotal role in his physical and mental recovery.

Kayla glanced at Jordan and Jasen, "You two working hard at the market for Mr. Kim?"

"Yes," Jordan assured her. "He said as long as we go to school, we can work for him!"

"He lets us have free snacks and one soda," interjected Jasen.

"I'm proud of you boys!" Kayla smiled, realizing Mr. Kim was helping her keep them off the streets and away from dangerous gangs. "Thank you for all your help getting Cameron back to school. It means a lot to have you two looking out for him!"

Kayla turned to Martin, "We haven't heard from you yet. What do you like about your class this year?"

"I love having our drums! Mrs. Carter is teaching us cool rhythms. Some days, we make a big drum circle around the room. She starts one group on a rhythm. The next group plays a different rhythm. Another group plays a third rhythm. We play our rhythms at the same time. It's so much fun. We only get drumming time if we work hard."

"That must sound awesome!"

"It does. Sometimes, I can hardly breathe!"

The conversation wound down. The boys cleaned up the kitchen and loaded the dishwasher. Kayla snuck off to her bedroom for some quiet time alone, reflecting on how her boys were doing. She was pleased with Cameron's resilience and determination to face the challenges of his recovery. The cardiovascular exercise involved in running would promote circulation, helping to improve blood flow and oxygen delivery to his healing tissues.

Engaging in track and field would also contribute to Cameron's physical rehabilitation by promoting flexibility and strength. Running involves a full range of motion for the legs and arms, enhancing joint mobility and preventing muscle stiffness. His overall conditioning from regular running would boost his endurance and energy levels.

It would be a powerful outlet for Cameron, participating in track and field. Running would relieve his stress, helping him manage the emotional toll of the recovery process. The rhythmic nature of running and the release of endorphins can alleviate feelings of anxiety or depression.

Being a part of the track team would give Cameron a sense of purpose and belonging. It would allow him to connect with his peers who share similar interests, providing him with a supportive environment. Kayla hoped the camaraderie and encouragement from his teammates would be instrumental in boosting his self-esteem and motivation.

Cameron would be setting and achieving personal running goals, empowering him. He would have control over his life, fostering a positive mindset. His progress on the track would enable him to reclaim his life after the challenges of burn recovery. Kayla was proud of his remarkable strength.

Meanwhile, George and Isaiah enjoyed a Sunday afternoon watching the Los Angeles Dodgers on their big-screen television. They relaxed in snug, well-worn recliners, sipping bright, pleasingly bitter Sierra Nevada Pale Ales.

George interrupted their serenity, "I stopped by Mrs. Carter's classroom. There was a good-looking man there who she said was a friend of their family and assisting her for the week. He gave me a bad feeling and stared right through me. He asked if I could put a deadbolt on her door. I got the idea he was a cop or had been a cop. He seemed to be snooping around!"

Isaiah tensed, "Did you get his name?"

"Yes, I looked it up on the visitor's sign-in sheet in the office, Neville Branson."

"I'll find out who he is! Did she say anything about her son?"

"She said he was home resting, and they were watching him for complications."

Isaiah's face looked strained, "We'd better find out why this guy is hanging around her! You need to stay away from her!"

"I kind of like her," laughed George. "I think I'm falling in love!"

"Fool!" retorted Isaiah.

CHAPTER EIGHTEEN

IT HAD BEEN A MONTH filled with many positive accomplishments for Tiffany's family. Bill's mother, Shirley, had proved a godsend during their crisis. She took excellent medical care of Austin, kept the house neat and clean, and cooked delicious meals. They were thankful for her love and support.

Austin made measurable strides in his recovery from the bicycle accident. His ribs had healed, enabling him to use crutches without extreme pain. His dad had returned the borrowed wheelchair. Shirley allowed his friends from the soccer team to visit and even fed them lunch. Austin would sit on the patio while they played basketball in the pool. They threw the ball to him. He would shoot, occasionally making a basket. Their visits lifted his spirits and encouraged him, giving him hope that one day he might be playing goalie again. The doctor would allow him to attend his team's soccer games as his condition improved.

Sidney had just returned from a week at volleyball camp. That evening, her family was planning their last dinner with Shirley before she flew back home to Seattle. Bill and Tiffany prepared a Tex-Mex meal, grilled skirt steak fajitas. Bill had marinaded the steak for five hours in the refrigerator. Then, he began his magic on the grill. Noses caught a whiff of beef, onion, garlic, and chili as the aromas wafted by on thin wisps of smoke and steam.

He placed a sizzling platter of tender meat and grilled peppers and onions in the middle of the table. Everyone had already picked out a soft, blistered, floured tortilla from the steaming stack in the warmer. The overwhelming, ultra-juicy, buttery steak melted in their mouths. It was accented by a slightly sweet and savory marinade, packed with lime and chili.

The conversation was lively between bites. Sidney told about the skills she learned at volleyball camp and the new friends she made. Tiffany talked about how her students progressed in their English reading and drumming. Other teachers were becoming interested in the results of the reading program she was teaching. They also saw the benefits of drumming on her students' behavior and mental health. She shared the drums with their classes, teaching them introductory rhythms. The music teacher ordered a set of drums for his classes. Bill was working on an important project that would improve the behavioral health services offered by Northeast Valley Health Corporation, expanding their various fields of expertise. Shirley was looking forward to getting back home. She missed her work at the hospital. She expressed her deep appreciation for the time spent with the family.

Everyone busied themselves, helping to clean up. Bill grabbed the empty platter, abruptly dropping hard back into his chair. The platter crashed onto the table. His hands clutched the arms of the chair. A confused look crossed his face as he blinked his unfocused eyes.

"Bill, are you okay?" his mom asked, alarmed.

"I think so. I felt dizzy for a moment."

Tiffany stepped out of the kitchen door, "What happened?"

"I just got a little dizzy," answered Bill. "I probably stood up too quickly."

Tiffany glanced at Shirley, "He's been having headaches in the mornings."

"When did you last have a physical check-up?" inquired Shirley.

"It's been a while!"

"Maybe it would be a good idea to make an appointment with your doctor," recommended Shirley.

"I'll make one on Monday," Bill promised. "My headaches are becoming more intense."

The next day, Bill and Tiffany said goodbye to Shirley at the Burbank airport. Tiffany's mom, Elizabeth, would be arriving in a couple of days to spend a month helping out. They were lucky to have such capable and available grandmas.

Neville had called the day before and asked if Tiffany and Bill could come to his home for an update. He had critical news to share with them. He had written a report of his findings on his computer. He wanted to share it with them, giving them a copy and a copy to the police. Detective Harris was in charge of the investigation at the Northridge Police Department. He was eager to know what dots Neville had connected.

Bill and Tiffany made their way down the sidewalk to Neville's home. It was a hot, uncomfortable summer day. All Tiffany could think of was how good a cool dip in the pool would feel. A heightened sense of unease filled their thoughts as they anticipated what news Neville had uncovered. They hurried their steps as they approached his front door. Knocking, they waited. There was no response.

"I'll check around back," said Bill, heading for the gate to the backyard.

"There's no sign of him," he came around the corner.

Bill knocked louder. Still no answer! "Let's call Detective Harris. Neville is not the type of person to forget an appointment."

They walked back home and called. Detective Harris picked them up in front of their house, driving them to Neville's home. He couldn't get any response either. Realizing something was wrong, he kicked the door in, breaking the lock.

"You two stay here."

Detective Harris cautiously entered the dimly lit living room, the air thick with an unsettling stillness. The room bore an eerie silence, disrupted only by the distant hum of traffic on a nearby busy street. A soft glow from the flickering overhead light revealed a scene that sent shivers down his spine.

Neville's lifeless body lay in the center of the room, sprawled on the threadbare carpet. His vacant eyes stared blankly into the abyss. A pool of crimson blood surrounded him, staining the once-beige carpet a deep, foreboding red. Detective Harris took a moment to steady himself, the gravity of the situation settling in as he surveyed the crime scene. His hands trembled as he checked Neville for any sign of a pulse. Harris called the police and then did a protective sweep. He searched the rooms for any sign to indicate that another individual was posing a danger to those on the scene. The creaking floorboards heightened his awareness. Chilling drafts brushed against his skin, evoking a growing fear as he looked for anything suspicious.

"Bill, Tiffany, come here," Harris yelled. "Neville has been shot!"

The three of them, shocked, surveyed the room. It exuded a disturbing mixture of metallic tang and the musty scent of aged furniture. The acrid odor of gunpowder lingered. A shattered vase lay nearby. The soft glow of a forgotten lamp cast long shadows across the walls. Faded family photographs adorned the walls, silent spectators to the macabre scene. Tiffany could not escape the palpable consciousness of sorrow that hung in the air. Neville's belongings lay scattered haphazardly around the room, attesting to the violence that had taken place. Her heart pounded in her chest. She shivered at the sudden temperature drops, feeling vulnerable in the threatening atmosphere. Bill put his arm around her, pulling her close. A creeping sense of dread spread over them as they grappled with the implications of the horror of this gruesome scene.

Closing his eyes briefly, Detective Harris took a deep breath, steeling himself for the challenging investigation ahead. He wrestled with alarm, struggling to maintain composure for Bill and Tiffany's sake. The room remained frozen, a graphic representation of tragedy that demanded justice.

CHAPTER NINETEEN

T HE POLICE ARRIVED AT NEVILLE'S house. They secured the area and began gathering evidence. Detective Harris drove Bill and Tiffany home. He interviewed them separately, piecing together what had happened leading up to Neville's death. Tiffany recalled the investigation at her school, the people he had met and questioned. He had been anxious to share the report of his findings with them and the police. He showed excitement about the relationships he had linked, possibly explaining the acts of harassment, terror, and revenge.

"I hope the police find Neville's report!" Tiffany asserted.

"I will call you later today," Harris assured her.

Tiffany's family sequestered themselves in their airconditioned home for the rest of the day. Bill put the security system on "alarm stay." Each was absorbed in their reflections and speculations. Tiffany felt small and insignificant against the overwhelming backdrop of Neville's brutal death. Sirens blared in the distance. She huddled into her cozy armchair, unsteady and shivering, feeling helpless and alone. Neville's investigation had given her hope. Now, he was gone!

Later that afternoon, Detective Harris called, "Hello, Bill, how are you all holding up?"

"Not very well! I think we're in shock!"

"I'm so sorry about Neville's death," Harris sympathized. "It's a great loss to our department. I will be here for you as we look for answers."

"Thank you," Bill said. "Any news?"

"I do have an update for you. Neville's computer is missing. There is no sign of a printed report. We did find a bullet lodged in the wall. I'll check his personal effects to see what clues I can find."

"We appreciate you keeping in touch with us!"

"I'll call you again tomorrow. Hopefully, I will know more by then."

Bill conveyed the update to the family. News of the missing computer and report startled them. They realized that unknown threats lurked around every corner.

Tiffany called the Los Angeles School District to request a substitute teacher to cover her classroom for two days. Bill decided to work on his project on the computer at home. Sidney would not go to volleyball practice until they made plans with Detective Harris.

Sydney kept busy cleaning the bedroom suite for Grandma Elizabeth's arrival. Tiffany did meal planning. Bill vacuumed, sitting down once in a while to rest. Austin hobbled around the house on his crutches, doing his least favorite job, dusting.

After dinner, Sidney and Austin preoccupied themselves with an ongoing chess game, absorbed in calculated strategic moves. Bill concentrated on his work project. Tiffany called Annabelle. She would stop by for a visit the next day to support and comfort her dear friend. Their family had survived the first day. Uncertain times lay ahead, frightening because of the awareness of danger.

Annabelle arrived shortly after breakfast the next morning, carrying a gorgeous bouquet of Tiger Lilies and a box of See's peanut brittle, Tiffany's favorite. After kisses on the cheek and hugs, they settled into a homey corner of the relaxing Water's Edge blue-painted living room. Tiffany told Annabelle the story of Neville's investigation, his spending the week with her at school, and the horror of finding him shot dead at home!

Tears welled up in Annabelle's eyes as she expressed her grief at the terror her friend was suffering, "You have my unwavering support. I hate that you're going through this! I'm just a phone call away."

"That means the world to me," Tiffany's voice wavered, her eyes moist.

She told Annabelle about how excited her class had been, learning to drum. She told her of the keen interest other teachers had expressed. She had been sharing her drums with them. The music teacher purchased drums for his classes.

"I'm so pleased," smiled Annabelle. "What a wonderful addition to their education!"

"I can't thank you enough!"

There was a knock at the front door. Bill asked who was there before unlocking it.

"Good morning," greeted Detective Harris.

Introductions were made and Annabelle said goodbye.

The family and Harris sat around the oval, oak kitchen table. The aroma of fresh-brewed French Roast coffee filled the room. Sidney had baked ultra-buttery, sweet, golden-brown scones. Bill nervously cut his scone, slathering it with strawberry jam, awaiting the latest news.

"I went through Neville's personal belongings," Detective Harris began. "He had wadded up a protein bar wrapper and a piece of paper in the pocket of a pair of pants. The paper had a name written on it, "Martin." Does that mean anything to you?"

"Well, I do have a student named, Martin," Tiffany observed.

There was silence as Harris considered this information. How could Martin be associated with Neville's cruel murder? Which dots had he connected?

"I would like to start with the names of your students, parents, and the staff at the school. Neville must have found some links, maybe one with Martin."

Tiffany's mouth fell open, her blue eyes round as saucers, "Martin has a beautiful family!"

"Often, we find secrets concealed behind closed doors, leading us to malicious motives."

"Is there something we can do to protect ourselves?" asked Bill.

"We should hire a security guard for Tiffany at school," Harris recommended. "I will work 24/7 on this case until we find Neville's killer!"

"Detective Harris," said Tiffany. "I have focused solely on protecting my family. Does Neville have any family?"

"Yes, we have contacted his daughter. She is on her way to make arrangements for the funeral and take care of the house."

"That should be a difficult job for her. Maybe we could be of help, living so close."

"I will let her know. Thanks!" responded Harris.

CHAPTER TWENTY

E LIZABETH'S ARRIVAL WAS A COMFORT to Tiffany, facing uncertainty and upheaval. Her mom's personality was warm, confident, and cheerful. The family needed her strength and loving care. She and Tiffany had a special bond, developed after her father had died. This would be an opportunity for Sidney and Austin to get to know their grandma in a deeper and more meaningful way.

The evening, before returning to school the next day, Tiffany sat visiting with her mom. She told her the story of the daunting events leading to Neville's death, and what difficulties she was facing at home and school.

"I don't want to go back to school tomorrow!" confessed Tiffany.

"You will be fine," reassured Elizabeth. "You have the inner strength to be there for your students. You can't protect everybody. Your independence and courage will empower your students and your family to face their challenges. I will be here to share in the responsibilities for the family. You will have a security guard outside your classroom door. We'll take one day at a time!"

"Thanks for your encouragement, Mom! I feel like I've lost control of my life!"

"Just let go. We'll work through this together. Keep up your journaling, meditation, yoga, and swimming. Believe in yourself!"

Early the next morning, the security guard showed up at Tiffany's front porch.

"Good morning, I'm Carl."

"We've been expecting you. I'll be ready shortly. Come in," Tiffany invited him.

Bill introduced himself and they had a quick cup of coffee together.

On their drive to school, Carl told Tiffany about his past career as a policeman in the San Fernando Valley.

"After retirement, I needed something useful to do," he said, fingers running through his thick, curly-gray hair. "I'm not one for sitting around the house!"

"I'm thankful for your help," said Tiffany. "You came highly recommended. Our family has found ourselves in difficult, dire circumstances."

"Put your mind at rest and concentrate on teaching your students. It will all work out. Detective Harris is one of the best."

Tiffany exited the freeway off-ramp onto Olympic Boulevard, heading to Leo Politi Elementary School. Palm trees towered overhead. Billboards crowded the sky. Businesses were still boarded up, looted, burned, ugly, and abandoned. She explained to Carl the anxiety and grief her students and their families had suffered. They had seen fires, looting, and army soldiers. They lived for weeks with the pungent smell of ash and smoke. All of them knew people in the community who had looted. The aftermath of the riots had left her students insecure and traumatized.

"We are in the process of healing," she explained.

"It's a long and difficult journey," Carl empathized.

Mateo waved to them as they arrived at the parking lot gate.

"Good morning, Mrs. Carter," he warmly greeted, as they exited the car. Marcela has missed you! I have an invitation for you and your family. She is going to have her first communion on Sunday."

"We would love to attend! Thank you for inviting us! Mateo, I'd like you to meet Carl."

"Nice to meet you," the men shook hands.

Mateo handed her the invitation, "Our family and friends will have a picnic after the ceremony. We would like you to join us."

"There will be five of us with my mother visiting," responded Tiffany. "We'll look forward to coming!"

Tiffany settled into her preparations for the school day while Carl surveyed the area he needed to watch. He developed a plan, identifying threats and vulnerabilities. His site inspection identified where the weaknesses were located.

The classroom door swung open. Carl walked in with George on his heels.

"This guy says he's a district maintenance man but has nothing to fix in your room!" stated Carl.

"It's okay, Carl, George is a friend. He often pops in to say "Hi" when he's on campus."

"Where's Neville?" George sniffed.

Tiffany hesitated, her face pale, "He was shot and killed in his home!"

"No!" George exclaimed in disbelief. "I'm so sorry!"

"Thank you, we're devastated at his loss!"

Carl stood, silently watching the interchange, "I think Mrs. Carter has work to get done before her students arrive!"

Carl directed George out of the door and closed it behind him, ignoring his angry look. George stomped down the walkway, mumbling to himself.

Meanwhile, Detective Harris had called Kayla and made an appointment to meet her at the beauty salon. Potted Palms were feathering out on either side of the entrance, softening the stark surroundings. A comfortable fragrant atmosphere greeted him as he stepped through the door. Kayla smiled and offered him a seat by her desk.

"I appreciate you taking the time to meet with me," Harris thanked her.

"What can I do for you?"

Harris described the events Detective Neville was investigating, leading up to his death. Kayla was astounded! She had not heard the news about what was happening to Mrs. Carter. Martin was happy and doing well in her class.

"I wanted to talk with you because a note was found in Neville's pants pocket. It had the name "Martin" written on it. The only "Martin" Mrs. Carter knew was your son."

"I don't have any idea what that could mean!"

"Would you tell me a little about your family?"

"Sure," Kayla agreed.

She told Detective Harris about her salon business and raising her family of boys. She told him where they went to school, where they worked, and how old they were.

"These incidents began happening to Mrs. Carter right after the riots," Harris informed Kayla. "It appears your salon survived the fires."

"We were very fortunate!" she expressed. "My son, Cameron, was in a fight during the riots. He was thrown into a burning store. He had treatment for his burns in the hospital for a month."

"I'm sorry to hear that!"

"He's better now, back at school and turning out for track and field."

"That's great! Does the boys' father live here too?"

"No, he left a few years ago. He lives in an apartment with his brother."

"Is he involved with the boys?"

"Oh, yes. He takes them out to eat on Saturdays. Sometimes he brings Cameron home from his after-school track practices and competitions."

"Where does he work?"

"He teaches physical education, and coaches basketball at Los Angeles High School on Olympic Boulevard."

"Kayla, thank you so much for meeting with me. I will let you know if I learn any new information."

"It's quite a shock to hear about Mrs. Carter. I hope everything turns out okay. Martin loves her dearly!"

Detective Harris began to see the dots Neville had likely connected. The next visit was going to be with the dad.

The school day went well for Tiffany and Carl. He joked around with the kids, winning their trust with his kindness. A large bouquet of pink roses was delivered to her classroom. Carl took it apart, checking the vase, water, and every flower. Then, he placed it on her desk.

Tiffany opened the note, "So sorry for all you are going through. Love from your friend, George."

CHAPTER TWENTY-ONE

Detective Harris drove from Kayla's beauty salon to the Los Angeles High School. Classes were done for the day. A secretary in the main office greeted Harris. He showed her his police badge and asked if Isaiah was still around.

"He is likely still in his office at the back of the gymnasium," she directed Harris.

"Thank you," he said, signing the visitor's check-in sheet.

Harris knocked on Isaiah's partially open office door. Hearing a gruff "come in," he stepped through the door into a brightly lit room. Basketball posters covered the walls; trophies lined the open shelves; and Styrofoam cups littered the desktop. A tall, muscle-bound man rose from his chair at the sight of a stranger.

"Hi, I'm Detective Harris with the Northridge Police Department. I was wondering if I could ask you a few questions?"

"Hello, nice to meet you," Isaiah turned on the charm. "What can I do for you? Please, have a seat."

"Thank you, I'll explain why I'm here."

Detective Harris went through the whole story again as he did with Kayla. Isaiah sat poker-faced, listening, and spellbound.

"You can see how Martin's name led us to Kayla and now, to you. She told me about Cameron's accident during the riots. Could you tell me the details of what happened?"

"The boys said they were swept into a crowd of rioters. The boys bounced a woman's car up and down at an intersection. Some guys tried to stop them and started a fight. Cameron was running away and fell through a broken window of a burning store. He was severely burned and spent a month in the hospital."

"I'm sorry to hear that," sympathized Harris.

"He's back to school, taking classes and running in track. Hopefully, that will help his self-confidence and road to recovery."

"Yes, it must be hard! Do you know who the men were who started the fight?"

"No, they just jumped out of a truck and attacked them."

"Do you know who the woman was in the car?"

"No, they had never seen her before."

"Well, thank you for your time. If I have any further questions, I'll let you know."

"You know where to find me," Isaiah grinned.

His grin faded to fury, his eyes blazing as he watched Harris walk away. He needed to get home and find out what George knew. He was going to stop by Mrs. Carter's classroom that morning.

Isaiah found it hard to obey the speed limit while driving home. The lights turned red as he approached. Traffic crawled. He hit the steering wheel as if it were to blame. He took deep breaths, trying to calm his racing heartbeat.

Isaiah slammed into the apartment, the door crashing into the entry wall.

"George!" he yelled.

"I'm in the bedroom. What's wrong?"

"Guess who came to see me today, Detective Harris!"

"Who's he?"

"He works at the Northridge Police Department."

"What did he want?"

"He wanted to know about Cameron's accident."

George stared at him in amazement, "Why was he asking you questions?"

"Detective Neville was shot and had the name "Martin" on a piece of paper in his pocket. Mrs. Carter said she had a Martin in her class. Harris went to Kayla's salon, asked her questions, and learned about Cameron's accident and me!" Isaiah exploded.

"Calm down and let's talk it over," George guided him to his recliner. "I'll get you a beer."

They silently sipped their beers, considering this latest development. Thoughts raced through their minds like a track with no finish line.

"The other night you got in late. Where were you?" George broke the tension.

"I went to Cameron's track meet. We decided to go out to eat afterward. It got kind of late!"

"Today, when I stopped by Mrs. Carter's classroom, a security guard was posted at her door! She told me about Neville being shot."

"Things are heating up! If the police question you, tell them I was home with you after dropping Cameron off."

"I will!"

Detective Harris sat at his desk in the Northridge Police Station. He had worked there for fifteen years. First, he spent five years as a patrol officer, gaining valuable experience. Then, he took a promotional exam to become a detective. The information he had gathered was spread out, randomly covering his desk. He analyzed it, making reasonable inferences from scattered details. Thinking "outside the box" was a valued skill. He used a whiteboard in front of his desk to organize his thoughts.

Harris picked a red marker for the dots. He drew the first dot in the center of the board at the top and labeled it, "Tiffany." He drew three black lines from Tiffany's dot, angling down to the middle of the board. At the end of each line, he drew a red dot, labeling the first one, "Mateo," the second one, "Martin," and the third one, "Jasen, Jordan, and Cameron." From Martin's dot, he drew three angling lines. Putting red dots at the ends of those connecting lines, he wrote "Neville" by one, "Kayla" by another, and "Isaiah" by the third. Last, he drew connecting lines from Kayla and Isaiah to Cameron, Jordan, and Jasen. Before him was a picture connecting the people involved so far.

Harris decided he needed to bring Isaiah in for questioning.

"Thank you for coming in," Harris began the interview.

"No problem," responded Isaiah.

"Where were you last Tuesday evening?"

"I went to Cameron's track and field competition. Afterward, we went to get burgers at In-N-Out. I dropped him off and went home to our apartment."

"Our apartment?"

"I live with my brother, George."

"Do you and George have weapons?"

"Yes, we both do. We were in the army together. They make us feel safer."

"Are they registered?"

"Yes."

"We recovered the bullet that killed Neville. I want to take a look at your weapons."

"That would be okay with me."

"Is George at home?"

"Yes, I think so."

"Would it be alright if my colleague and I follow you home?"

"Sure."

Detective Harris and Sergeant Miller followed Isaiah to his apartment. George met them at the door, surprised to see the police.

"They want to see our weapons," explained Isaiah.

After introductions, Harris asked George, "Where were you last Tuesday night?"

"I came home after work and was here all night."

"Was Isaiah here too?"

"No, he went to Cameron's track meet. They had something to eat and he dropped him off at Kayla's. Then he came home."

"What time was that?"

"About eleven o'clock."

Harris and Sergeant Miller checked the weapons and registrations. They thanked the brothers for their cooperation and left.

In the quiet of the car, Harris confirmed, "It was a 22-caliber bullet we recovered from the scene at Neville's house. Isaiah and George own 9mm guns!"

CHAPTER TWENTY-TWO

IT WAS A SPLENDID MORNING. Tiffany's family were dressed in their conservative Sunday best for Marcela's first communion. The eleven o'clock Spanish-speaking Mass would be at Saint Peters Catholic Church near Leo Politi Elementary School.

Sidney and Austin had never been in a Catholic sanctuary. They walked down the center aisle with awe, taking in the magnificent, intricate stained-glass windows and grand arches. A floor-to-ceiling image of Christ crucified framed the altar in the front. The atmosphere was serene, filled with a sense of joy and celebration. Near the front of the church, the children, alongside their families, gathered to receive the Eucharist for the first time. The ceremony was usually held in May but had to be delayed due to the disruption of the riots.

Marcela attended a year of catechism classes where she learned the significance of the Eucharist, the meaning of Communion, and the rituals involved. Before first communion, she partook in the sacrament of Reconciliation (Confession) to seek forgiveness for her sins and purify her soul.

Tiffany, Marcela's teacher, shared the joy of this milestone. She exchanged smiles with Marcela and her proud parents, Mateo and Sara. Marcela's long black curls shone against her fancy, white dress and veil. White symbolized purity and her commitment to Christ. The church was adorned with gold and white decorations.

The ceremony began. Hymns echoed through the nave. The scent of incense lingered in the air. The proceedings were heartfelt as the congregation witnessed the reception of Holy Communion. First, the priest consecrated the bread and wine. Then, the children received the Eucharist which Catholics believe is the body and blood of Jesus Christ. Sidney and Austin observed the sacred occasion with deep reverence and wonder.

After the communion, the congregation spilled out into the warm Los Angeles sunlight. They exchanged hugs and words of encouragement. Tiffany hugged Marcela and slipped a congratulatory card into her hand.

Marcela's family arranged a post-communion gathering at a reserved pavilion in a nearby city park for a festive lunch with family and friends. Vibrant flowers bloomed around the grounds, and the sound of children playing made it a lively and celebratory atmosphere. Tiffany and her family joined everyone, where tables were adorned with beautiful floral arrangements. Buffet tables were loaded with beef tacos, Mexican corn salad, bacon and cheese-stuffed Jalapeno Poppers, Tex-Mex wings with salsa, mini quesadillas, tamales, pork carnitas, and nachos. In the center of the table was a lovely, pink-icing cake with the words "Marcela's First Communion."

After lunch, the children played—climbing, sliding, and swinging. Marcela noticed a man strolling along a winding path with a cute little dog. It was adorable, small in stature with fluffy fur. It bounded alongside its owner with an infectious enthusiasm. Its tail wagged happily, and its ears flopped playfully as it explored the surroundings. Marcela had always wanted a pet dog and couldn't help but be drawn to the endearing sight, smiling and saying "Hello" as they passed. His ears perked up and his tail wagged with excitement as she approached. The man told her it was okay to pet the dog. It strained and tugged on the leash, pulling it out of the man's hand. It went running down the path along the ravine.

"Help me catch him!" the man yelled to Marcela.

She and the man ran down the pathway. They rounded a corner. The dog was stopped, sniffing at the bushes. As they came to a stop, the man bumped Marcela over the edge into the ravine. A terrified scream brought the parents and children running. They looked down in horror at Marcela's body crushed on the rocks below. Her face was caked with dirt. Blood smears ruined her beautiful white dress.

The festive atmosphere shifted to one of panic and concern. People shouted frantically, searching for ways to help. Mateo and some of the other men scrambled down the steep hillside. Marcela was not responding to them calling her name.

"Someone, call 911!" Mateo yelled to the crowd gathered along the edge of the ravine.

They heard the sound of sirens wailing in the distance. Emergency services rushed to the park. As the ambulance arrived, the once cheerful pavilion became a scene of worry and apprehension. Marcela was carefully loaded into the ambulance, surrounded by concerned faces. Mateo and Sara went with her, depending on family and friends to pack the food and decorations.

The ambulance sped away, leaving behind a stunned gathering. Thoughts and prayers filled the air as everyone headed home, anxiously awaiting news from the hospital. Tiffany and her family drove home, grappling with the uncertainty of Marcela's well-being. They were overwhelmed with dread and disbelief. Tears streamed down Tiffany's face. She had an unsettled feeling about Marcela's dangerous fall.

With a voice choked with emotion, she asked the question on everyone's mind, "Was Marcela's fall an accident, or was she lured into a trap?"

CHAPTER TWENTY-THREE

T HE LAST WEEKS OF NOVEMBER flew by. It was a sad time for Tiffany's class. They missed Marcela. She spent a week recovering in the hospital with a minor concussion, a broken left arm, a broken ankle, and numerous cuts and bruises. Her mom, Sara, was caring for her at home. Tiffany stopped by every few days to visit and keep Marcela up to speed with her schoolwork. The police interviewed people attending the celebration at the park for her first communion. No one seemed to remember seeing a man walking a dog.

Carl was keeping a close watch on Tiffany at school. Detective Harris met with her family, explaining how his investigation had led to Martin's family. She was horrified and alarmed to find out that it was Kayla's boys who had attacked her during the riot. It was distressing to know Cameron had suffered severe burns, feeling maybe it was her fault. The connection to Isaiah and his brother, George, was even more shocking. Harris explained his thoughts on the family wanting revenge. George could be connected to the bloody skull on her car, her keys and her driver's license moved to a different pocket in her purse, and the slashed drum heads.

Detective Harris had included Carl in the group so he would be aware of the findings. Isaiah and George might have felt threatened by Neville's investigation. It might have been Isaiah and George who ran down Austin on his bicycle. They would have known her address from her driver's license. George was getting information from Tiffany at school and knew Neville was getting close. That would account for him being shot. However, the brothers' weapons did not match the recovered bullet. Isaiah had an alibi for that evening and night, being with Cameron at a track meet and home later with George.

Tiffany was blindsided at the news of the connections between the three young men, Kayla, Martin, Isaiah, and George. Outrage consumed her, realizing George had used her, pretending to be her friend.

She was startled with a frightening thought, "Could they be responsible for Marcela's accident?"

"Yes," exclaimed Harris. "That has already crossed my mind! On my whiteboard at work, I have all the connections to you from the incident during the riot. I already had Mateo connected. I drew another line from Isaiah to a dot. I labeled it, 'George.' "

"I'm scared to see George again! It's appalling to think he could deceive me like that! He never told me he was related to Martin!"

"Carl will be with you every minute, so that should deter George from stopping by to see you or causing any trouble."

The school day ended with a rousing drum circle. Carl was joining in now, enjoying every minute of second grade all over again. The students were all smiles as they met their parents at the gate.

As Tiffany and Carl walked past the office, the secretary stuck her head out of the door, "Tiffany, there's a delivery for you at the service gate."

"For me?"

"Yes, for you."

They made their way to a truck parked at the back of the school. Annabelle's husband, Grayson, jumped down from the passenger side.

"Hi, Tiffany," he greeted in his sophisticated English accent. "We have a surprise for you!"

"Wait a minute!" Carl rushed up.

Grayson beamed, "Annabelle said other classes were interested in drumming so she bought one hundred drums for us to deliver! Your principal okayed it and has a storage area ready for us!"

"I need to inspect the truck first!" Carl informed him.

"Carl, I'd like you to meet my best friend's husband, Grayson. Grayson, this is my security guard, Carl," Tiffany introduced.

"Great to meet you, Carl! I hear you are doing an awesome job!"

"Thanks, now, let me check the truck!"

As Carl ensured the truck and its load were safe, Grayson walked over, giving Tiffany an all-encompassing hug, a little too tight and a little too long.

"We missed you at the office when you left for your teaching job!"

"It has been wonderful getting together with Annabelle! This is an amazing gift! I can't thank you enough!"

"Thank Annabelle. It was her idea! I approved, of course!"

The unloading was done. Grayson said goodbye with another overly exuberant hug. The truck driver handed her the delivery receipt for the drums.

"I think Grayson's sweet on you," observed Carl.

"Wow! Can you believe it! One hundred drums!" Tiffany ignored him, excited.

Arriving home, she shared the delight of receiving Annabelle's drums. Everyone was stunned at such a generous gift. Dinner on the patio was light-hearted. Austin was wearing a boot, making it easier to get around school. He attended soccer practices and even played goalie a little. Bill had his doctor's appointment and tests. They were waiting for the results. Elizabeth's month was almost completed. She had been a much-needed support for the family and a confidante for Tiffany. Sidney had volleyball games which they all loved watching. Her specialty, of the six positions on the team, was the setter. She had a delicate touch, setting the ball perfectly for the attacking players.

Bill and Tiffany had a relaxing swim. They headed in for an early night. Bill showered while she got comfortable in their seating area overlooking the serene landscape lighting. She pulled out of her school bag the receipt for the load of drums. She smiled, amazed. There was a note with it, proba-bly from Annabelle. As she unfolded the piece of paper, her heart began to race. Scrawled hastily in jagged handwriting, the words seemed to leap off the page, sending a chill down her spine. She steadied her hands. It was a threatening message, filled with venomous words that seemed to burn into her consciousness. For a moment, she felt frozen. Cold sweat broke out on her forehead, her mind unable to process the shock of what she was reading. It ended with, "Prepare, you have not seen anything yet!"

Bill emerged from the bathroom to see his pale, wide-eyed wife, a paper crumpled in her hand!

CHAPTER TWENTY-FOUR

DECEMBER ARRIVED, RAINY AND COOL. The brown hills in the distance had turned light green with the welcomed moisture. Tiffany and her class were out of school for the month. It gave her time to prepare for Christmas without the usual rush.

As she sipped her steaming coffee, thoughts of the threatening note raced through her mind. She shared it with Detective Harris. He was tracking down the delivery truck driver to find out if he knew its origin. Taking a deep breath, she considered her life of risks and uncertainties. One thing was certain. She would not let fear dictate her actions. She sat up and straightened her shoulders with a sense of purpose, determined to face whatever challenges lay ahead. Whoever had sent that venomous note would soon realize they had picked the wrong person to mess with.

Christmas would be different this year. Normally, they would be joined by family from Seattle. Tiffany wanted to get away and have Christmas up north with them this year. But it was not to be. They met with Bill's doctor to discuss the implications of his test results. They showed a benign tumor located in the cerebellum, the lower back part of the brain that controls coordination. It was slow growing.

It explained Bill's headaches, loss of balance, and fatigue. The doctor explained the symptoms that would progress and worsen over time as the tumor grew. There would be muscular difficulties with walking and weakness on one side of the body, causing trouble with precise movements of the hands, arms, and legs. There would be trouble swallowing, and problems with speech rhythms. Bill could experience blurred vision, dizziness, confusion, and seizures. The only cure was surgical resection. They would begin with treatment to shrink the tumor and slow its growth. With Bill's mom's nursing specialty in this area, she recommended the UCLA Health Brain Tumor Center. Bill would receive the most medically advanced treatments there. The center was known for its leading-edge research.

Christmas would be low-key. The kids would likely spend time with friends. The only big event they would attend as a family would be a lavish New Year's Eve party. Annabelle and Grayson invited them to their beautiful home overlooking the Pacific Ocean for an evening of celebration. It was a special time to look forward to. Tiffany and Sidney would start planning what everyone would wear for the elegant occasion.

By evening, the sun had come out. The kitchen was cleaned after dinner. Bill and Tiffany were ready for a swim. Just as she was about to dive into the pool, she noticed something unusual at the bottom. Curious, she dove in, reached down, and pulled it out.

"What is this!" Tiffany exclaimed, unzipping the water-tight bag.

Inside was a small velvet box.

"I'm sure I don't know!" Bill grinned mischievously.

She gasped as she opened it, "A ruby necklace!"

"Surprise! I thought you deserved something special for all your hard work!"

"It's breathtaking! Thank you!" she hugged and kissed him passionately.

She laid the necklace on the table, admiring the center ruby, with its deep crimson hue and intense brilliance. It glimmered in the sunlight, surrounded by a halo of sparkling diamonds. The chain was intricately crafted and polished to perfection. Along the necklace, clusters of smaller rubies were interspersed among the diamonds, each with a unique shade and characteristic. They seemed to come alive as the light danced across the surface of the rubies.

Tiffany took Bill into her arms, holding him close, "Thank you, my Sweetlove," she whispered, tears in her eyes.

The first family, to begin their Christmas traditions, were Mateo, Sara, Marcela, and Mateo's brother and cousins. Sara and Marcela decorated their home with elaborate scenes depicting the birth of Christ. On December 16, they began a nine-day reenactment of Joseph and Mary's search for lodging in Bethlehem. Each evening, the family gathered to pray, sing carols, and meet at a different house every night. Traditional Mexican food and treats were served. On Christmas Eve they had a festive meal together. They ate Bacalao (salted cod stewed in a sauce), tamales, Pozole (a hearty soup), Bunuelos (thin fried dough sprinkled with sugar and cinnamon), and Atole (a warm, thick drink made from corn dough, flavored with cinnamon and vanilla). After the meal, the family attended Midnight Mass to celebrate the birth of Jesus. On Christmas Day, Mateo's family exchanged gifts and enjoyed another festive meal with the extended family.

Over at Kayla's home, she had decorated their dining table for the Kwanza celebrations. She placed a woven mat in the center, putting a candle holder in the middle. She placed a black candle in the middle holder, then three red candles on the right side of the black candle, and three green on the left. She arranged four dried ears of corn. Each one represented Jordan, Jasen, Cameron, and Martin. They symbolized the parent's wish for them to grow up strong and happy. Fresh pears completed the arrangement. On December 26, they began the celebration of seven guiding principles known as the Nguzo Saba. On day one, they lit the black candle of Umoja (Unity). They reflected on that principle and discussed its meaning for their family and community. Day two they lit a red candle, Kujichagulia (Self-Determination). Day three they lit a green candle, Ujima (Collective Work and Responsibility). It went back and forth until they had lit the seventh candle. The number four candle was Ujamaa (Cooperative Economics). The number five was Nia (Purpose). The number six was Kuumba (Creativity). The number seven was Imani (Faith). On the last day, January 1, they feasted on catfish, collards, macaroni and cheese, jerk chicken, gumbo, rice and black beans, and black-eyed peas. They gave each other educational or artistic, homemade gifts. Isaiah and George joined them, bringing a skateboard for each boy. They had made them at the woodshop at the high school where Isaiah taught. Each board had his name painted in fancy calligraphy.

Tiffany's family was getting ready for Christmas. She and the kids decorated the house, making it festive. She put so many lights on the tree that they hardly had any room left for the decorations. Christmas Eve, they honored Tiffany's family traditions with a ham, baked potatoes, and green bean casserole dinner. There was Christmas Pudding with lemon sauce for dessert. They opened a few gifts. Christmas morning, they honored Bill's family traditions with Santa bringing more gifts. They munched on leftovers and fancy cookies for the day.

To their delight, New Year's Eve was a gorgeous sixty-six-degree day. They arrived at Grayson and Annabelle's opulent home, the picture of extravagance and luxury. They were greeted at the door by the hosts themselves, Grayson, tall, with thick dark hair, distinguished graying at the temples. He welcomed them with his smooth English accent. His deep, liquid brown eyes exuded warmth and charm. Annabelle was radiant in her elegant emerald party gown. Her neck was adorned with a mesmerizing, dazzling emerald pendant. Its lush green hue gave an aura of refinement. Diamonds enhanced the necklace's overall allure with their shimmering light. She was the picture of glamour, her silvery-blond hair coiffed to perfection.

Annabelle's eyes lit up when she saw Tiffany approaching, "You look divine!"

"Thank you! You look enchanting!"

Tiffany looked resplendent in a crimson gown that complemented her ruby necklace. Her reddish-blond hair cascaded down her shoulders, framing her striking blue eyes with an air of elegance.

Beside her stood Bill, his rugged features softened by a warm smile. With sandy-brown hair and piercing blue eyes, he carried himself with quiet strength. His cane supported him, a testament to his determination and resilience.

Sidney took in her surroundings as they entered the mansion, amazed at the grand architecture. Her blue eyes sparkled with excitement. She wore her long blond hair with youthful exuberance, attracting wistful attention.

Austin observed the festivities with curiosity. Tall and shy, his athletic build contrasted with his reserved demeanor. He was not entirely accustomed to the extravagance of the occasion.

The atmosphere was lively and sophisticated. Guests mingled amidst tastefully arranged hors d'oeuvres tables, where gourmet delights tantalized the senses. Shimmering trays offered an array of delicacies, from freshly shucked oysters to bite-sized wagyu beef sliders, complemented by artisanal cheeses, charcuterie selections, and decadent truffle-infused appetizers.

Champagne flowed freely throughout the evening, with servers circulating amongst the crowd, ensuring that glasses were never empty. In one corner of the room, a string instrument group serenaded with melodic tunes, their music drifting through the air like a gentle caress. The soothing notes provided a perfect background for conversation and laughter, enhancing the ambiance of the gathering. Grayson and Annabelle circulated among the guests, ensuring every detail was attended to with precision and grace.

As the night progressed, the tempo picked up, and the spacious ballroom transformed into a dance floor. Couples swayed gracefully to the rhythm of live music. Their movements were illuminated by the soft glow of twinkling lights and the moonlight streaming in from panoramic windows overlooking the ocean.

Bill and Tiffany sat watching the night unfold, filled with laughter, music, and joy.

She felt a tap on her shoulder, "May I have this dance?"

Bill looked lovingly at Tiffany, "Of course!"

Grayson and Tiffany glided away. Annabelle sat by Bill's side, "They look wonderful together!"

The music was delightful. Tiffany danced with beauty and grace. Grayson led her around the floor and the corner of the L-shaped room. When Bill and Annabelle were out of sight, he pulled her close.

"You are ravishing tonight, Tiff!"

"Thank you," she tried keeping some distance between them.

"You know I've loved you since you walked through my office door!"

"But how could you! Annabelle is smart, accomplished, and beautiful!"

"She is, but I can't get you out of my heart and mind. Do you think someday you could love me?"

"You know I love Bill! I'm devoted to him!"

"I would give you anything you wanted!"

"Yes, but the most important thing I want is Bill's love for me."

"He's a lucky guy!"

As the clock ticked close to midnight, the air filled with laughter, the clinking of glasses, and the gentle sounds of waves crashing against the shore below. There was joy and anticipation, an unforgettable start to the year ahead.

CHAPTER TWENTY-FIVE

Tiffany and Carl drove down Olympic Boulevard toward Leo Politi Elementary School. Along the way, businesses were rebuilding. Fewer stores were boarded up. New signs appeared in the windows. Many received financial assistance after months of red tape.

They prepared the classroom for the first day of getting back to school in January. The second graders bounded in, filled with excitement to be back. Carl was almost as enthusiastic as they were. He bonded with the children and was dedicated to protecting Tiffany.

A deep voice boomed, "Good morning, Mrs. Carter!"

Mateo stood at the door, pushing a beaming Marcela in a wheelchair.

"Good morning! Did your family have a good Christmas?"

"Yes, we spent lots of time with family, eating!" he laughed.

They got Marcela settled at her desk. When it was time to meet to share on the corner rug, everyone wanted to push the wheelchair. Tiffany made a sign-up sheet so they could take turns.

The Djembe drums had been distributed to various classrooms. Teachers shared, rotating teaching rhythm, coordination, and cultural appreciation. They found it a powerful tool, allowing students to express emotions non-verbally. The rhythmic patterns and beats served as a release, helping to channel energy and reduce stress, anxiety, and tension. Engaging in drumming required the students to focus and concentrate on the rhythm. This focus, on the present moment, helped reduce stress by diverting their attention away from worrisome thoughts. Drumming has been linked to lowering levels of cortisol, the hormone associated with stress. The act of playing triggered relaxation responses in their bodies. The repetitive motion and coordination involved stimulated various areas of the brain. Endorphins were released, promoting a sense of well-being.

The goal was to train the students to participate in group drumming sessions or drum circles. This communal experience reduced the feelings of isolation, promoting unity and support among participants.

The school community at Leo Politi Elementary had experienced trauma and distress during the riots. They tore apart their neighborhood. Drumming offered a multi-faceted approach to stress relief, combining physical, emotional, neurological, and social elements. It promoted team-building. The use of Djembe drumming spans all cultural, social, and musical settings, making it a beloved and versatile percussion instrument.

It had been a joyful reunion for Carl, Tiffany, and her classroom of students. Carl wheeled Marcela to the pick-up line at the gate, assuring Mateo that she had done well and had a good day.

Kayla walked toward them. Martin hugged her, getting a big kiss in return. Three young men stood behind her. Carl protectively stepped next to Tiffany.

"Mrs. Carter, I'd like you to meet my three sons. Jordan is the oldest, and this is Jasen, and then Cameron," Kayla introduced, pointing them out.

"I'm happy to meet you," Tiffany's breath caught in her throat.

Jordan shook her hand first, "I want to tell you I'm sorry for attacking your car and ask if you will forgive me!"

Tiffany stood, stunned. A smile reached her lips, "Yes, Jordan, I forgive you!"

"Thank you!"

Jasen stepped around Jordan, shaking Tiffany's hand, "I am very sorry too! Will you forgive me?"

Now the smile had reached Tiffany's face and eyes, "Of course, Jasen, I forgive you too!"

Cameron stepped close, tightly grasping Tiffany's hand, "I'm very sorry for what I did to you! Will you forgive me?"

Tears filled her eyes, "Yes, I forgive you, Cameron! I'm so sorry for what happened to you!" She placed his hand between hers.

"Thank you!" he teared up. "I'm running in track now. I would like to invite you to my track meet on Saturday at the Los Angeles High School."

"I would love to come!" she squeezed his hand. "My whole family will come!"

"Thank you!"

Martin could not contain himself, jumping up and down, "Goodbye, Mrs. Carter. See you on Saturday!"

Kayla and Tiffany exchanged smiles, knowing huge steps had been taken in her boys' lives. They said "Goodbye," faces reflecting relief and happiness.

The week was busy for Tiffany's family. Bill still worked at his office until his treatments began. Sidney and Austin concentrated on their schoolwork and sports practices after classes.

On Saturday, as promised, Tiffany and her family sat in the stands at the track field at the high school. It was cooler weather, perfect for running. Cameron spotted them and waved. Kayla, Jordan, Jasen, and Martin joined them on the benches. She introduced her boys to Tiffany's family.

"You kids sit together and get to know each other," she suggested.

Martin wanted to sit beside Tiffany. She scanned the stands, noticing a man sitting alone. As the track meet progressed, she fidgeted with her hands and kept looking over her shoulder. Bill sat on the other side of Martin, enjoying his enthusiasm. Sidney sat between Jordan and Jasen. Austin sat on the other side of Jasen. Jordan thought he had never seen anyone as pretty and captivating as Sidney. He watched her eyes sparkle and her ponytail bounce up and down as she talked. They discussed their classes, teachers, and sports. Austin and Jasen had a common interest in soccer. They discussed the strategies of the game and the positions they played. Jasen asked why Austin was wearing a boot. He shared the story of his bicycle accident. The boys were horrified to hear it was a hit-and-run.

They all cheered for Cameron. He finished a strong second place in the last race. They congratulated him. He thanked Tiffany for coming and was introduced to her family.

Martin gave him a big hug, "You ran so fast!"

They said their goodbyes and promised to attend another track meet soon. Jordan watched Sydney walk away, eyes full of admiration. Tiffany walked briskly to the car, feeling uneasy and vulnerable.

On the top bench of the stands, a man sat wearing a jacket, cap pulled down over his face. Carl would not take Tiffany's safety for granted, not in enemy territory! His vigilant gaze scanned the surroundings for any potential threats. Anything could happen in such an open setting.

Hidden in the score booth, Isaiah looked on, eyes flashing, clenched fists, consumed with uncontrollable hatred. His body trembled under the weight of his animosity. He would have to intensify his plans for revenge!

CHAPTER TWENTY-SIX

THE SAN FERNANDO VALLEY ENJOYED a refreshing change in weather with cooler temperatures. The dawn broke, the sky a canvas of soft hues, transitioning from deep purples and pinks to a vibrant blue. Sidney and Austin felt invigorated by the crisp air carrying a slight chill as they spent their school day walking from class to class. Despite the cooler temperatures, the sun still shone brightly. Fragrant citrus orchards filled the air with their sweet aroma. After school, they hung around for a while chatting with friends.

The streets of Northridge buzzed with the usual activity as cars navigated through the maze of roads. Sidney drove, with confidence, behind the wheel of her Toyota Camry, her focus unwavering as she made her way home. A pleasant breeze was blowing through the windows. On the passenger side, Austin was telling her the news of the day. Approaching an intersection, she put on the blinker and moved into the left-turn lane. A car screeched to a stop next to them at the red light. Austin looked over and saw a gun pointed out of the back window.

He whipped his head around, yelling at Sidney, "They've got a gun!"

"Get down!" Sidney screamed at him.

The blast of a gunshot split the air. She spun the car into a U-turn. With a squeal of tires, the other car followed, tailing them with intent.

Austin peered around, "You've been shot! Your arm is bleeding!"

"Get down!" she demanded as another shot rang out.

The once-peaceful streets transformed into a battleground. Sidney was caught off-guard by the sudden pursuit. She accelerated, weaving through the traffic. Another gunshot shattered the back window.

"Drive faster!" Austin urged, his heart racing with fear and adrenaline.

Sirens wailed in the distance as their pursuer's aggressive maneuvers became increasingly dangerous. They barreled through intersections, narrowly avoiding collisions with oncoming traffic. Sidney drove with skill and precision. Despite the chaos unfolding around them, she remained composed, determined to shake off their assailant.

The chase was becoming desperate. She made a split-second decision. She veered off the main street, darting into a labyrinth of side streets and alleys. Being familiar with the neighborhood was to her advantage. The pursuing car followed, hot on their trail! Austin could see blood running down Sidney's arm, soaking her clothes and the seat. She did not seem to notice as she maneuvered the car, her grip firm on the steering wheel.

"Head to the police station!" he commanded.

"We're almost there!"

With each twist and turn, they edged closer to their destination, the local police station. Sidney's eyes flickered with determination, her resolve unyielding. One final burst of speed brought them skidding to a halt outside the station. The pursuing car slammed on the brakes at the edge of the parking lot, realizing where they were. Making a quick turn, the car sped away.

Breathless and shaken, Sidney and Austin emerged from their car. Their hearts pounded with relief as they ran to seek refuge within the sanctuary of the police station. They had successfully outmaneuvered their pursuer.

Officers swarmed the scene. Seeing that Sidney was bleeding, they called an ambulance. The paramedics assessed her injured arm and provided emergency care. They reassured her it was a flesh wound but would need follow-up at a medical facility. They stopped the bleeding and bandaged it. She wanted to wait for her parents to arrive to make any decisions about where to go for treatment.

Meanwhile, Detective Harris appeared. He questioned Austin, getting the story of their terrifying chase. He would talk to Sidney after she had reunited with her parents and had medical attention.

When Bill and Tiffany arrived, Sidney fell apart in their arms, crying softly. The horror of their escape began to sink in. Her parents listened with trepidation as Harris explained the gunshots and the harrowing chase that ensued. He told them about the flesh wound that needed to be treated.

Detective Harris tried to comfort the distraught parents who were in shock. Apprehension overwhelmed them as they realized the violence that had occurred against their children. Harris accompanied them to the clinic. Sidney's car was evidence and was left at the station to be investigated. Her eyes darted back and forth as they settled into Tiffany's car. Her tear-stained face reflected the emotional turmoil swirling around inside her.

Sidney felt a sharp stinging sensation when the wound was cleaned. It was treated with an antibiotic and bandaged. The doctor would continue to check for infection and give her a tetanus shot. It would take two weeks or longer to heal enough to uncover the wound. He gave her medication for the throbbing ache of her arm.

Detective Harris stayed behind Tiffany's car as they drove home. His sharp eyes scanned for any cars following. He made a phone call when he had the family secured in their home.

"I hired a security guard! He'll be here tomorrow morning. Meanwhile, I will guard the house tonight." Harris told them. "I don't want anyone going out tomorrow, so you must make necessary arrangements."

No one was hungry, but Tiffany made grilled cheese sandwiches to compliment her homemade Roasted Tomato Soup. She ladled it into warm bowls, trying not to spill with her hands shaking. She garnished them with Parmesan and basil. Harris joined them around the kitchen table. He said a blessing, thanking God for keeping Sidney and Austin safe! There was a solemn silence as they ate. The atmosphere was strained.

Austin's nervous voice suddenly burst out, "You should have seen her drive! She drove like the devil was chasing us!"

Everyone laughed, relieving a little of the tension.

"Maybe he was!" murmured Bill, his jaw clenched.

With a furrowed brow, Harris headed outside for guard duty, struggling to maintain his composure, feeling the pressure of protecting the family he had grown to admire.

CHAPTER TWENTY-SEVEN

Tiffany's family stayed home for the week after Sidney and Austin's chilling car chase. Detective Harris brought groceries and took Sidney to her doctor's appointment. Her arm was healing nicely. He also took Bill to the UCLA Health Brain Tumor Center for his first treatment.

It was Tiffany and her second-grader's month off from school. She needed critical time to rest and regroup. During her break, she would prepare for the last two months of her students' school year. She settled into her cozy chair by the living room gas fireplace. It flickered on low, taking the chill off the room. She was startled at a shadow moving outside the window, then realized it was the security guard.

Floorboards creaked as Bill came into the room, joining her. Every sound made her heart race with dread. He sat across from her facing the comforting fire.

"How are you feeling?" asked Tiffany.

"Much better! I had a great sleep! The doctor said I can go back to work in two days."

"Good! I wish I wasn't so jumpy!"

"It's understandable with all we've gone through."

"I'm so thankful we have each other!"

"Do you think we need some counseling for the kids and us? It's difficult to deal with our lives being threatened!"

"That's a great idea!"

"I'll look into it at work and research who would relate best to our family."

Bill returned to work the next week, and Sidney and Austin returned to classes. Tiffany used the quiet time productively, writing lesson plans and reviewing her students' progress. Thoughts crowded her mind, disturbing her peace. Bill's health troubled her. She remembered how devastating the loss of her dad was when she was young. It would tear her apart to have her kids go through the same agony. It was frustrating having so much of life out of her control.

Bill was due for another treatment. It went well and he was resting at home for the day. Tiffany decided to make a quick run to the store. She let the security guard know where she was going. Getting out of the house felt good. She took deep breaths in the fresh, cool air. She cautiously drove out of the neighborhood, checking the rearview mirror. She took her time picking out groceries, savoring a little freedom.

Returning home, Tiffany carried her bags down the side of the house to the back kitchen door. Setting them on the counter, she began putting them away. The house was still. She had an uneasy feeling. Ripples of fear coursed through her veins.

"Bill," she called.

An eerie silence hung heavy in the air. Something was not right! She stepped cautiously out of the kitchen, noticing the front door slightly ajar. Alarm bells went off in her mind. She ventured farther into the room. The first thing that caught her eye was the security guard, lying on the floor, unconscious and bound. Tiffany's heart raced as she rushed to his side. She saw blood oozing from the back of his head. He was breathing and had a strong pulse.

She felt a sense of dread gripping her as she realized the gravity of the situation. Her gaze darted around the room, her eyes landing on Bill. He was bound and gagged. She ran to him, untying the gag with shaking hands.

"Bill, are you alright?"

A look of confusion and fear distorted his pale face, "I think so."

Tiffany struggled to maintain composure, reaching for the phone and dialing emergency services as quickly as possible. Every second felt like an eternity as she waited for help. Her senses heightened to the slightest sound or movement. She sat on the floor, cradling Bill, comforting him. The room was in disarray, with furniture overturned, and belongings scattered haphazardly. It was evident someone had forcibly entered, leaving chaos in their wake. Tiffany's mind raced as she tried to comprehend what had happened and who could be responsible. Emergency services arrived and the paramedics went to work assessing Bill and the security guard for injuries. The guard was stirring and moaning, fighting to wake up. Putting them securely in the ambulance, they left for the hospital.

Tiffany called Detective Harris. The police arrived, beginning their preparations to start investigating. Harris took Tiffany to school, picking up Sidney and Austin. They were shocked to hear the story of the invasion. Harris explained that their home was the scene of a crime. They were perceived as being in danger so he arranged for them to stay in a Safe House for a few days.

They arrived at the hospital and found Bill sitting in his bed in the emergency room, waiting for them. Tiffany hugged him and gave him a loving kiss.

"Glad you're okay, Dad!" exclaimed Sidney. "Did they hurt you?"

"My wrists hurt where they tied me up!" he massaged them.

"They tied you up!" Austin gasped, a horrified look crossing his face.

"They gagged me too!"

"When we have you settled in the Safe House, I'll interview you both," Harris looked at Bill and Tiffany.

"A Safe House?" asked Bill.

"We'll be investigating the crime scene so I want you in a secure place for a few days."

Bill was silent. Frightening thoughts swept over him like a huge rouge ocean wave. The terror of being tied up, helpless, seared into his brain. He pulled the warm blanket around his neck, suddenly chilled and shaking. The doctor gave him medication to calm him and help him sleep. Otherwise, he was allowed to leave with his family.

Detective Harris drove them to the Safe House. It blended into the neighborhood, surrounded by hedges and large established trees. He pulled into the driveway, stopping to punch a code into a panel. The gate slid open. A camera monitored their approach to the house. It was a plain-colored, sprawling rambler with grey shutters. Harris turned off the security alarm as they entered the front door. The great room had overstuffed, sink-into couches and a large television. They looked around, taking in the spacious dining room and well-appointed kitchen. Harris led them down the hallway to the two bathrooms and three bedrooms. There were all the comforts of home.

Detective Harris sat them on the comfortable couches. He gave them instructions, "The phone is only to be used for emergencies or calling me. Stay inside the house for now. I will bring a nurse in to check on you tomorrow. We are going to go day by day, assessing your need for protection. I'll stop by your house and bring clothes and personal items. I'll pick up some groceries too. All your basic supplies, like soap, toothpaste, toothbrushes, and towels, are provided. If you want to talk to a counselor, I can have one here tomorrow. Do you have any questions?"

"Not now," responded Tiffany.

"You will be safe here, so don't be anxious. Try to relax. I'll set the alarm when I leave and be back soon!" Harris assured them.

The door shut behind him. The dazed family sat quietly looking around at their temporary environment.

"Dad, what happened?" asked Austin.

"I let the security guard in to use the bathroom. While he was in there, two men with guns burst through the door. One found the guard and must have knocked him out. He dragged him into the living room and tied him up. The other guy tied my hands and ankles and gagged me. After that, I could hear them crashing and banging around the house. They left carrying bags stuffed full."

"I wonder what they took," mused Tiffany.

"I'm so sorry!"

"It's not your fault, Dad!" snorted Sidney. "It's the stupid security guard's fault!"

They sat in silence again. Life had taken a sinister turn. It was difficult to remain positive under such extreme mental strain. The strange, unfamiliar noises in the house made them jumpy.

"Let's watch TV," Tiffany suggested.

"Would you mind if I lie down to rest?" inquired Bill. "I'm exhausted!"

They distracted themselves by watching Roseanne and The Addams Family. Tiffany checked on Bill. He was sound asleep.

CHAPTER TWENTY-EIGHT

T HE DAYS IN THE SAFE House crawled by like turtles in a race. Detective Harris brought homework for Sidney and Austin, Tiffany's school bag, and Bill's computer. He worked on the dining table and the others worked in their bedrooms. Harris brought a nurse who checked Sidney's arm and everyone's blood pressure and vital signs. A counselor spent a morning, meeting with them as a group and individually. They were a tough bunch—strong and resilient. Tiffany led them in Yoga exercises to reduce stress and keep them healthy. It relaxed them and gave them some control of their body and breath.

Detective Harris gave them an update on the progress of the investigations. No witnesses had identified the car in the shooting and chase. The bullet that shattered the back window of their car was found embedded in the front seat. It had not come from Isaiah's or George's weapons. They also had alibis for the time of the chase.

The robbery investigators had found no clues yet. They wanted the family to go home and write down what was missing. Usually, robbers took cash, jewelry, weapons, televisions, stereo equipment, and computers. The investigating team would let certain organizations know what to look for, pawn shops, taxi drivers, small store owners, bars, and gas stations. Most property was never recovered.

Sidney and Austin looked around in dismay at the chaos and destruction in their home. A feeling of vulnerability swept over them. They began searching the bedrooms first for missing items.

They heard Tiffany cry out, "My ruby necklace, it's gone!"

"I'm so sorry!" Bill embraced her.

"I loved it! You gave it to me!" she said, tears in her eyes.

They made lists of missing items to give Harris. It was a substantial financial loss for the family when added to the damage to the furniture and accessories. The day was filled with straightening up and cleaning.

There were now two security guards, one in the front of the house and one in the back. The guard they had during the robbery invasion was recovering in the hospital.

The weather was warmer. Tiffany served dinner at the patio table. The freedom made them feel like they had been let out of prison. They took a welcomed, relaxing swim in the pool. The evening gave them a new appreciation for the sunset and the sparkling glow of the exquisite landscape lighting. They soaked up the calm and serenity, happy to be back home.

Life seemed normal again in the weeks that followed. Bill's doctor's appointment revealed that the treatments had not shrunk his brain tumor. He recommended surgery as soon as possible. Bill called his mom to see if she could care for him when Tiffany returned to school.

Bill's mom, Shirley, wanted to be with him for the surgery, so Sidney prepared her room. They all went to pick her up at the airport. It was the farthest they had driven from home for a long time. Hillsides and yards were filled with California poppies, unfurling their deep orange petals. Cherry tree flowers formed clouds of blushing pink blooms against the clear blue sky. The beauty cheered their hearts, giving them hope for a bright future.

Bill's surgery was a success. The surgeon assured them that he had removed all of the tumor. It was a week before he could be moved home to recover under Shirley's skilled nursing care.

Tiffany returned to Leo Politi for the last two months of her school year. Her second-grade class was reading and writing well in Spanish and English. She had immersed the Korean students in English. They were thriving. Carl still kept a close watch, protecting her.

The music teacher wanted to try their first school-wide Djembe (ZHEM-bey) drum circle in the courtyard. The principal approved it and plans were made. Students placed chairs in circles, radiating out from the center from where the leader would direct. The Djembe drums were first used for the king of Mali. They communicated from mountain to mountain that the king was arriving.

Students with drums filled the chairs. The remaining ones sat along the walls of the garden beds. Mr. Lopez, the music teacher, stood in the middle of the circles. He had them warm up, to loosen their muscles, with basic Djembe rhythms. Before starting, he established the ground rules of a drum circle and showed them the non-verbal signals he would use.

Annabelle and Grayson were invited. He brought a drum to participate with them. Annabelle stood to the side, intently watching the proceedings.

The drumming began with Mr. Lopez using the call-and-response technique. He played a rhythm on his drum and then the drummers echoed it back. He gradually increased the complexity of the rhythms as the students became more comfortable and confident. As the circle progressed, he guided the group dynamics by modulating the intensity and tempo of the drumming, leading transitions between different rhythms. He was skilled at using verbal cues, hand gestures, and body language to engage the group and keep them focused.

Mr. Lopez felt they were ready for a grand finale. He divided them into three groups, teaching each one a different rhythm. When they had mastered it, he signaled everyone to start drumming. The loud, rich, deep sound of over one hundred Djembe drums soared into the air, filling the courtyard, spilling over the walls, and beyond into the neighborhood. People stopped what they were doing and listened to the glorious sound.

Annabelle was swaying to the music. Soon, she danced freely as the rhythms led her body and soul. The students sitting along the walls joined her, moving gracefully around the courtyard. Their faces were filled with joy as they danced to the enthralling beat of the drums.

Mr. Lopez gradually let them wind down the drumming and signaled the conclusion. The dancers stopped, clapping and cheering. He thanked everyone for contributing to the drum circle, celebrating a sense of community and connection. It had been an uplifting musical experience for all involved. It had been healing.

In the Bambara language in Africa, Djembe means "Everyone, gather together in peace." The message was sent throughout the Leo Politi neighborhood, instead of mountain to mountain as in Mali, business to business and home to home. What better call to action for a community recovering from a devastating riot? Their children would lead the way.

CHAPTER TWENTY-NINE

T HE SCHOOL YEAR WAS OVER for Tiffany and her second-grade class at Leo Politi Elementary. She planned an awards presentation for her students and their families. They lined up at her classroom door to be approved by Carl. The office had checked them all, but he was double-checking. The students wore their best outfits, suits, and fancy dresses. The parents were loaded with gifts of appreciation. This time, it was not just flowers and food but fine jewelry, Mexican dresses, casual wear, chocolates, a Korean tea set, a book bag, lantern candles, Spanish artwork, choice wine, and a gift basket filled with coffee, cheeses, sweets, olives, plantain chips, mugs, and a cookbook.

Tiffany presented students with an award, congratulating each on their hard work and tremendous progress over the last two school years. She told the parents what each child had contributed to the classroom community. She praised their maturity, personal growth, and dedication to learning. Parents beamed with pride, hearing about their child's accomplishments. The class made a drum circle to end the celebration. It was a brilliant performance.

Carl and Tiffany received handshakes and hugs as parents left with their children. Mateo's family and Kayla were the last to leave. Mateo and Sara thanked her profusely for teaching Marcela and even coming to their home while she was recovering from her fall. Kayla tearfully thanked Tiffany for her gracious forgiveness of her boys and for teaching Martin to love reading.

It took a while to load all the gifts. Carl and Tiffany drove to her home, overwhelmed with the outpouring of love they had received. Carl was taking a much-needed break, flying to Belize for a diving trip on the barrier reef. After Austin and Sidney finished their classes, Tiffany and her family flew to Seattle, Washington, and north to Bellingham to stay for a getaway in a cabin near Mount Baker.

Bill's mom, Shirley, and his dad, James, owned a log cabin on Silver Lake in Maple Falls, Washington. The Mount Baker ski area was a twenty-six-mile drive away. They drove down a gravel driveway, lined with giant Douglas fir trees. The cabin appeared in a clearing on the edge of a picturesque mountain lake. A hemlock dock jutted out from the shore. Kayaks and canoes were strapped to the dock. It had a small seating area with chairs facing the view of the regal North Cascade mountains. Mount Baker rose majestically as the "star of the show," a beautiful, ice-capped peak, bold and distinctly visible across Puget Sound and into Canada. The kids ran to the dock, thrilled with the beauty of their surroundings. They were excited to settle in and begin their explorations and adventures on the pristine waters of the lake.

After unloading the car, Tiffany got Bill comfortable in a chair by the water's edge, wrapped in a warm blanket. He was recovering from brain surgery and would be able to participate in gentle activities. Right now, after their long trip, he needed to rest, soaking in the calming sights and sounds.

Tiffany looked in the kitchen cupboards, finding what she needed to fix dinner. Shirley had generously stocked them and the refrigerator. She made a quick delicious spaghetti dish, livening up the jar of sauce she found with red pepper flakes, a pinch of parsley, and a dash of salt and pepper. Baby spinach was in the fridge to make a salad, adding toasted walnuts, sliced Granny Smith apples, cheese, dried cranberries, bacon bits, and Honey Dijon dressing. While she made the salad, the sauce and noodles simmered in a pan, and garlic bread warmed in the oven.

They ate dinner on the expansive deck, stunning views in every direction. For some reason, their meal had never tasted so delicious. The cool, mountain air lifted their spirits as they anticipated the abundance of outdoor activities in the area. This was a perfect retreat for the family to relax, recharge, and nurture their bond amidst the natural splendor of the Cascades.

They slept peacefully on their first night in the cabin. Bill and Tiffany took the downstairs bedroom while the kids slept in bunk beds in the loft. Austin was the first up in the morning. He tried his hand at building a fire in the river-rock fireplace. He remembered watching a survival program on TV, showing the best way to build a fire was like a log cabin, not a tent. That formation burned the wood slower and so the fire lasted longer. Bill praised Austin's Boy Scout skills as he made the coffee. Tiffany and Bill prepared breakfast. They reminisced about their camping trips when they were first married. They laughed about the time at Lake Louise in Canada when mosquitos swarmed them, filling their eyes, noses, and mouths. They could not get the tent set up, so the only room they could find available was at a beautiful resort on the top of a mountain. Another time while they were tenting, a sudden flash flood washed them away from their campsite. The kids laughed to hear the stories. At Silver Lake, they were making new memories with their children. They were thankful for the opportunity to disconnect from their recent stress.

Tiffany showed Austin and Sidney how to get into a kayak from the dock without tipping over. The three paddled along the shore, enjoying the variety of cabins and homes. Bill rested on the dock in the peaceful ambiance of the surroundings, fostering a sense of well-being and rejuvenation. Later, he would walk with Tiffany on the trails weaving through the woods, surrounding the cabin.

They looked forward to a trip up Mount Baker. Tiffany packed a lunch and they headed up the mountain. The road to Artist Point was still buried in thirty feet of snow, so they parked at the Heather Meadows Visitor Center. They admired the incredible scenery from the viewing area, guarded by Table

Mountain. Below was the sheltered basin, home to Bagley Lakes. Bill found a comfortable spot in the visitor's center while the rest hiked the two-mile loop around Bagley Lakes. They were amazed, not only by the views but also by the serenity and timelessness of the basin. The patchy snow created incredible designs and textures on the already surreal landscape. There were still a few snow patches to cross on the trail. Waterfalls serenaded them along the way. There were fun bridges to cross, the trail following alongside a stream carrying snowmelt from Table Mountain. Wildflowers poked through the thawing ground. It was simply beautiful.

Before leaving the center, they sat at one of the picnic tables to eat their tasty tuna and egg salad sandwiches. Their final stop was at Picture Lake where Mount Shuksan was reflected in the smooth water. Bill got out and walked the short trail around the lake. A sense of peace came over him. He was grateful to be alive and spending time with his family. It was a perfect day, blue sky, sunny and warm with lingering patches of snow.

Shirley and James drove up to visit them at the cabin. They stayed the night on the sleeper bed by the fireplace. James barbequed hamburgers for dinner. The kids shucked the corn-on-the-cob which he roasted on the BBQ. The seclusion and privacy allowed them to disconnect from the hustle and bustle of everyday life. James and Austin lit the fire pit after sunset. They made smores and warmed their hands with mugs of hot chocolate. They laughed and talked into the night, creating cherished memories for the family to treasure, a priceless gift from Shirley and James.

CHAPTER THIRTY

T IFFANY AND HER FAMILY WERE home in Northridge after a fabulous trip to Washington State. Bill went to work two days a week, building back his stamina. Sidney and Austin enjoyed having friends over for games in the pool. They also had sports camps to attend. Sidney was perfecting her skill as a setter on her volleyball team. Austin was playing goalie for his soccer team. Sports camp would help him rebuild his confidence and hone his skills.

Tiffany faced the challenge of beginning a new school year with a first-grade class. It was important for her to remain patient, flexible, and supportive as the children learned to adapt to the new expectations of first grade.

On the first day, she began with orientation activities to help them become familiar with their new classroom, classmates, and teacher. She introduced classroom routines, using fun games and stories. The kids were excited, easily losing their focus. Some of them struggled with transitioning from the more relaxed atmosphere of kindergarten to the structured environment of first grade.

By the second day, Tiffany began establishing daily routines such as morning meetings, circle time, and transitioning between activities. The challenge was helping the students understand the importance of following these routines while allowing flexibility and understanding their need for breaks. Some of them exhibited behaviors such as talking out of turn or getting easily distracted, disrupting the flow of the day.

As the week progressed, Tiffany started introducing academic expectations. Some children struggle with developmental differences at the beginning of first grade. She differentiated her instruction to meet the diverse needs of the students, ensuring that everyone was making progress.

Socialization was an increasingly important aspect of her classroom as the children began to form friendships and navigate peer interactions. She facilitated group activities and collaborative learning experiences to promote social skills, such as sharing, taking turns, and resolving conflicts. She intervened when a few disagreements occurred, teaching appropriate ways to communicate and interact with others.

It was an exciting and challenging week. Tiffany relaxed on the weekend with her family. She and Bill swam each evening, enjoying the warm summer weather. They always had their best conversations while soaking in the hot tub. Bill told her about his taxing week, and getting back to work. His expectations had been too high, so he decided not to push himself, slowing down. Tiffany recalled her demanding week of training a new class. Her tension subsided with the tranquilizing massage of the hot tub jets. They settled back, shutting their eyes, quieting their thoughts, yet well aware of the security guard making his rounds.

The next day Tiffany reflected on what worked well with her new class and what needed improvement. She adjusted some classroom routines, balancing academic instruction with social-emotional development. It was a rewarding experience that would set the tone for the rest of the school year.

Each week, Tiffany saw the children adjusting and improving by leaps and bounds. She washed the sink and Carl straightened up the classroom at the end of another successful week when the phone rang.

"Hello," Tiffany answered.

"Mateo is here. He wants to come to your classroom. Would that be alright?" the secretary asked.

"Sure, send him down." She turned to Carl, "Mateo is on his way."

A somber Mateo with a furrowed brow entered the door.

Seeing his distress, Tiffany asked, alarmed, "Mateo, what's wrong?"

He sat down with them, telling them about the tragic events of the day. His construction site was bustling with activity that morning. The workers were diligently carrying out their tasks. Metal clanged against metal. It was loud and noisy, with the whirr of machinery and shouts of instructions. Scaffolding had been built, providing workers access to the various levels of the half-constructed building.

Suddenly, without warning, a loud crack shattered the din on the site. The scaffolding buckled and swayed before collapsing in a cascade of metal bars and wooden planks. Dust and debris filled the air. A worker plummeted, his body twisting in mid-air before crashing to the ground with a sickening thud. Nearby workers rushed to his aid, frantically clearing debris to reach him. It turned out to be one of his cousins. The family was with him at the hospital.

"I'm so sorry!" expressed Tiffany, dismayed.

"What do you think happened?" Carl asked in horror.

"I don't know. Yesterday, I inspected the scaffolding and it looked fine!"

"What could go wrong?" asked Tiffany.

"We have been using this scaffolding for a while and it was strong. We regularly maintain it. The workers have been trained in the safety rules. My cousin was always careful not to overload the scaffolding with his equipment and materials. My men and I have been talking today. We don't think it was an accident! I checked it last evening. I did not see anything that needed repair. My workers have been going through the debris. They think there may have been some loose brackets. One board is slick with oil and grease. My cousin wasn't using any grease or oil. No one went up before he did."

Tiffany's mind raced, "Someone sabotaged it during the night!"

"Have you reported it to the police?" Carl asked.

"Yes, they are investigating now."

"I'm going to let Detective Harris know about this!" exclaimed Tiffany. "Is there anything we can do to help?"

"No, I'm going to the hospital. First, Marcela gets hurt, and now my cousin!" Mateo's angry voice rose, his fists clenched.

"These incidents could be connected to Tiffany's attack during the rioting and your rescue and fight with the young men," deduced Carl.

"Yes, I thought of that!"

Tiffany hugged Mateo as he left, "Let us know what we can do to help your family!"

Carl paced back and forth across the room, running his hand through his hair in exasperation. He sighed, frustrated, "You are all in great danger!"

They were quiet on the drive to the San Fernando Valley, both fearful of the frightening implications for Tiffany's and Mateo's families. Whoever was on a path of revenge was not giving up. Assaults were ramping up, becoming more frequent and more violent. They were in a fight for survival.

CHAPTER THIRTY-ONE

MATEO'S CONSTRUCTION SITE ACCIDENT HAD left Tiffany tense and anxious. A threatening shadow hung over her head, a thundercloud, ready to burst. Her nerves were frazzled. She hoped the month of September at home would help to settle her restlessness and uneasiness. What could happen next? Her life was spiraling out of control.

Austin and Sidney were beginning a new school year. Sidney's senior year of high school was filled with planned special events, senior pictures, senior car parade, senior breakfast, senior night, senior skip day, and graduation. She applied for the University of Washington's "pre-health" program. She was accepted. The process included actively exploring a variety of healthcare professions to learn how different types of work might match her strengths, motivations, and preferences. It would be an exciting new chapter in her life.

Annabelle called, wanting to take Tiffany out for a shopping trip and lunch. She jumped at the chance for a pleasant day out with her friend. Annabelle picked her up at the house and drove to the iconic and glamorous Rodeo Drive shopping area. It was located in the heart of Beverly Hills, stretching for three blocks.

"I can't afford to go shopping here!" remarked Tiffany, taking in the elegant architecture.

Rodeo Drive was lined with Palm trees, meticulously maintained lush greenery, and colorful flower beds. Buildings were adorned with beautiful facades, marble columns, and ornate details. The atmosphere was luxurious.

They left the car in a parking garage and began walking down the block. Annabelle took Tiffany's arm and led her to the captivating window display of the Gucci store.

She pointed to the handbags, "Your purse is old and worn out. We'll pick out a new one today, a gift from me!"

They entered the store and found themselves surrounded by luxury and refinement. The interior design was lavish with sophisticated furnishings.

A middle-aged, elegantly dressed woman approached them, "How may I assist you today?"

"We are shopping for handbags. Tiffany is a teacher, so we need a bag to carry her school materials, an everyday purse, and a clutch purse for dressy occasions," responded Annabelle.

Tiffany looked surprised at the list of handbags but knew better than to say anything. They were given brand information, style advice, and impeccable service. They left with the most beautiful leather handbags she had ever imagined.

Annabelle led her to an exquisite restaurant for Al Fresco dining. They sat under a chic umbrella, the perfect setting for people-watching and enjoying the California sunshine. It was a great location for celebrity spotting. Lunch was a decadent affair. Annabelle ordered a starter, delicately diced fresh Ahi tuna mixed with avocado, cucumber, and a tangy citrus dressing, served atop a crispy wonton shell. The dish was garnished with microgreens and drizzled with a wasabi aioli for a hint of heat and creaminess. It was served with a crisp Chardonnay.

During lunch, they talked about what was going on in their lives. Tiffany told about their family's rejuvenating trip to Washington and staying in a log cabin on a lake.

Annabelle could not imagine such a trip, "That sounds like a perfect place to relax and unwind. We always go to lavish resorts. I'm still worn out when we get home from the whirlwind of activities and parties."

The main course was flawlessly served. A perfectly grilled USDA Prime filet mignon was cooked to their preferred temperature and served with a rich red wine reduction sauce. Truffle mashed potatoes, sauteed wild mushrooms, and roasted heirloom carrots for a harmonious balance of flavors and textures, complimented it, along with a bold Cabernet Sauvignon.

As they savored the main course, Tiffany told her about the accident on Mateo's construction site. "It seems like we are being targeted. The attacks are becoming more dangerous!"

"Maybe you should come stay with us for a while where you'd be more protected!"

"Thank you, but we have to go to work and school. We have two security guards at the house now and Carl goes to school with me."

"I wish I could do more to help!"

Dessert arrived, decadent molten chocolate cake with a gooey chocolate center, served warm with a scoop of Madagascar vanilla bean ice cream and a drizzle of raspberry coulis. The combination of rich chocolate, creamy ice cream, and tart raspberry created a luxurious and indulgent dessert experience, accompanied by a sweet Riesling.

They relished their time together, stretching lunch out as long as possible. Annabelle drove them home, chatting about their successful company and exciting trips to the Santa Anita horse races. Grayson loved to bet on his favorite thoroughbred horses. Tiffany wondered how they could be best friends and live in such divergent worlds with distinctive realities.

While Tiffany spent her month off relaxing and writing lesson plans, Isaiah and George were making plans too. George had heard that Mateo's cousin was in the hospital with spinal injuries.

"I don't know how these people continue to survive!" Isaiah complained, his face flushed, veins bulging in his neck. "It seems like they have 'nine lives.' "

"Maybe God sent a guardian angel to protect them!" suggested George.

"You're crazy! Nonsense!" Isaiah exploded, clenching his fists. "We'll see about that! Tiffany will not live to see another Christmas! Here's the plan!"

CHAPTER THIRTY-TWO

T**IFFANY FELT RESTED AND READY** to tackle another two months of teaching her first graders. They were more mature now than in the first two months. They knew the expectations and school routines. It was time to begin Tiffany's reading program, half a day immersed in Spanish and the other half in English. By the end of these months, the students would start reading. It was exciting for them and their parents.

Tiffany began drumming with her new class, teaching them to focus and follow directions. Learning the basic techniques and rhythms was beneficial for their coordination development. They learned to respect one another's space and follow the established rhythm. It became their favorite part of the day.

The first week went well. Tiffany was glad for the weekend, attending one of Sidney's volleyball games and spending time with Bill.

"How's it going at work, Sweetheart?" she asked him, as they relaxed on the chaise lounge chairs beside the pool.

"Great. My project is almost complete. Everyone is looking forward to the expansion of our mental health services!"

"That's a great accomplishment! I could use those services right now!" she laughed.

"You seem a little tired after your week back to school."

"The kids are progressing well but keeping them on track is a lot of work! I always forget how little they are when they begin first grade!"

"Well, I'm giving you more time to unwind. I'll cook one of your favorite Indian dinners, Chicken Saag!"

"Thank you! I'll play a piano concert for you while you cook!"

Bill got to work in the kitchen, grating the ginger and garlic. He thinly sliced the onion. Getting out the slow cooker, he set it on high. He cut the chicken cutlets into one-inch pieces and seasoned them with cumin, turmeric, garam masala, salt, and pepper, placing them in an even layer in the cooker. Then, he made a tomato mixture, whisking together tomato paste, cornstarch, and water. He warmed it in the microwave. After that, he added coconut milk, chicken stock, curry powder, ginger, garlic, and onion. Mixing that, he added more turmeric, cumin, garam masala, and sugar. He poured the sauce over the chicken and covered the cooker for one-and-a-half hours. After that, he tore spinach into the pot and added cashews, stirring to combine. As he worked, he smiled with pleasure. Tiffany was playing one of his favorite piano concertos. He made the rice while the spinach cooked in the sauce for thirty minutes. Before serving, he stirred creme fraiche into the chicken saag. Last, he divided the rice into bowls. He topped it with the chicken saag and added lemon wedges.

The family ate on the patio, delighted with the Indian-inspired meal, slow-cooked for rich complex flavor. Their schedules had gotten busy again, so this was a welcomed downtime together.

"Thanks for the wonderful concert!" Bill appreciated.

"Thanks for the delicious dinner!"

Tiffany was enjoying her class more as they settled into learning. After another week, Carl and Tiffany cleaned the room. The custodian did a thorough job of vacuuming, emptying the garbage, and cleaning their bathroom. There was a sink with a drinking fountain that she scrubbed and Carl straightened up the room and materials.

"Carl, would you please drive home today? I've developed a splitting headache."

"Sure. You've been working too hard! Try to get a good rest this weekend!"

As the next weeks went by, Tiffany's headaches increased and she began having stomach pains.

Bill noticed, "Are your headaches getting more frequent?"

"Yes, I think it's all the stress at work and not knowing if something terrible will happen to one of us or Mateo's family!"

"Let me know what I can do to help!"

"Thanks. I think I'll lie down for a while. I feel nauseated."

The next week at school, Tiffany was feeling sick, vomiting a couple of times.

"Why don't you take some sick leave and go to the doctor," Carl recommended.

"You know me," she laughed. "I never like to miss school."

"You need to take care of yourself!"

After their usual routine of cleaning up the classroom, Tiffany looked at Carl, "I'm having chest pains!"

She paled, gasping for air. Carl ran to her as she collapsed onto the floor. He tapped her shoulder. There was no response. He made sure she was breathing okay. Then, he phoned the office to call for an ambulance. Her eyes flickered.

"Help is on the way," Carl reassured her. "Try to breathe slowly and deeply."

Carl continuously monitored her breathing and pulse. When the ambulance arrived, he provided the paramedics with as much information as he knew. They assessed her condition. They administered oxygen therapy through a mask and attached a cardiac monitor for signs of a heart attack. Based on their findings, the paramedics determined to transport Tiffany to the hospital for further evaluation.

As they loaded her into the ambulance, from a dark, deserted classroom across the parking lot, two eyes watched. With a racing heart, he hurried, letting himself out of the service gate.

Carl called Bill, letting him know the situation. Bill could meet them at the hospital. The doctors and medical staff conducted a thorough clinical assessment.

Meeting Bill and Carl in the hallway, the emergency room doctor stated, "Her heart is strong. She is not having a heart attack! I have a few questions for you. Does she take any medications?"

"No," answered Bill.

"How has her health been recently?"

"She's been complaining of headaches, stomach pains, and nausea in the last few weeks," Bill's voice trembled.

"Today, before she collapsed, she said she had chest pains," said Carl.

The doctor turned to him, "Who are you?"

"I'm Carl, her security guard at school."

"Security guard?"

"Yes, her life has been threatened!"

The doctor thought for a minute, "I'm going to order blood and urine tests to look for certain toxins, drugs, or chemicals. We may be dealing with a poisoning. I'm going to consult with our toxicologist. Carl, I would like you to go back to her classroom. Bring anything you can find for me, vomit, things she touched, medications, lotions, cleaners, aerosols, and any containers from what she drank and ate today."

Carl spun around without a word, rushing to the exit doors. The doctor abruptly left to order the toxicology tests. Bill stood in the hallway, alone, and in shock. A nurse led him to a chair in Tiffany's room, seating him securely. He felt disoriented and panicked, bombarded with beeping monitors, harsh lighting, and the acrid smell of disinfectant.

The Forensic Toxicology Team decided to administer antidotes based on her symptoms, even before the laboratory results were available. Her vital signs were stabilized. They treated her with medications to control her nausea and vomiting.

Bill's thoughts and emotions churned like a violent sea. Tiffany appeared ashen-faced. Helpless and fearful, he could only watch her distress. Who would poison her? How? Icy fingers of dread squeezed his heart. He could not endure the painful thought of losing her, the love of his life!

Suddenly, the monitors began screaming an ear-piercing alarm! Medical staff rushed into the room!

"She's having a seizure!"

CHAPTER THIRTY-THREE

THE HOSPITAL ROOM WAS A whirlwind of activity. Tiffany's body convulsed with violent tremors, her eyes rolling back into her head as she gasped for air. Panic gripped the room, their voices blending into a blur of urgency. Bill felt his chest tighten with alarm as he watched helplessly, his mind racing with a million fears. He wanted to reach out, to comfort her but was paralyzed by the sight of her suffering. The medical team worked quickly and efficiently, stabilizing Tiffany as best they could. Bill could only watch, his heart heavy with the weight of uncertainty.

As the seizure subsided, her breathing was labored, but steady. Bill felt a rush of relief wash over him. But beneath it all lingered a deep sense of unease, knowing that his wife's life hung in the balance. Her fate was uncertain until the toxicology results came back. With a heavy heart, he gently took her hand in his own. His eyes filled with tears as he whispered words of love and encouragement, praying for her strength and recovery.

Carl walked through the door with Sidney and Austin following. Their mom lay on the hospital bed, her once vibrant face now pale and drawn. The monitors beeped incessantly. Their dad sat, holding her limp hand, his face radiating fear. He slowly rose, hugging them tightly. Carl had filled them in on what happened to their mom at school.

Sidney walked around the bed, taking her mom's other hand, "Austin and I are here, Mom. We love you!"

She thought she felt a weak squeeze but was not sure. Austin stood by her bedside as if frozen to the spot. His heart ached as he watched his mom lying there, so vulnerable and fragile.

The emergency room doctor walked in, introducing himself to Sidney and Austin. He led the family and Carl into an empty room nearby.

"Toxicology blood tests showed abnormal blood clotting, so we are beginning treatment for anticoagulant rodenticide intoxication. She is being given vitamin K1 and a plasma transfusion to supply coagulation factors. She may need long-term treatment with vitamin K1. She needs supportive care in the hospital, including IV fluids for severe dehydration and treatments for disrupted brain activity, headaches, and nausea. Her prognosis is good because she is strong and healthy. She will need home care until she gains her strength back. Have a wheelchair ready for her since she will be too weak to walk yet. Do you have any questions?"

"Do we know if it was rat poisoning?" asked Carl.

"Toxicology is testing the items you brought in. Her symptoms reflect rat poisoning. It is a common poison since it is easily accessible. Once we know for sure, you might want to alert the police."

Carl brought sandwiches in for everyone as they waited by Tiffany's side. She had briefly opened her eyes and given them a faint smile. Any small sign was encouraging. They discussed how to care for her when she came home for recovery. Austin suggested asking her mom, Elizabeth if she could come down again. He had grown quite attached to her when she cared for him after his bicycle accident. They all agreed that would be a great thing for their family. There was a week left of Tiffany's two months on track. A substitute teacher would fill in for her. Then, it was December, her month off. Maybe Elizabeth would stay through Christmas and her husband could come down to join them.

As they made plans, they heard a whisper, "You people need any help with your planning?"

"Yes, Sweetlove!" Bill grinned with relief. "We didn't mean to leave you out!"

They hugged her and Bill leaned over the bed, giving her a tender kiss on the forehead. Soon she was resting peacefully, eyes shut, breathing softly.

Toxicology did find rat poison. It was in the cleaner Tiffany used to clean the classroom sink. Carl left to call Detective Harris. Bill called Elizabeth who would fly down at the end of the week. He would not leave Tiffany's side, so Austin brought food from the hospital cafeteria to keep them going. By the end of three days, the doctors were confident of her recovery. The kids went back to school. Bill left to check on their home and pick up a wheelchair from work again. He hoped this would be the last time they would need it!

The next week, the family settled into a new routine. Elizabeth was unpacked and busy efficiently running the household. Tiffany rested in bed, sleeping a lot. She struggled to eat, so her mom made custard and foods easy to digest. She made sure Tiffany was taking her medications and vitamins. Bill appreciated her loving care of their family.

That weekend, Bill brought home a Christmas tree. Everyone was delighted as they gathered in the living room. Austin wheeled his mom in and placed her in a spot where she could enjoy the decorating. Sidney put on Christmas music. As twinkling lights flickered to life on the tree, the cozy living room radiated with warmth and love. Bill stood tall beside the tree, his hands carefully arranging ornaments with Austin and Sidney. Cheerful laughter filled the air as they reminisced about each ornament's story.

Austin reached up, placing a shiny star at the top of the tree while Sidney carefully hung delicate glass Baubles. Bill grinned proudly at his children, his heart swelling with joy at seeing them working together.

Meanwhile, Tiffany sat in her wheelchair nearby, her face glowing with admiration as she watched her family bond over the holiday tradition.

Despite her weakened state from the poison that had nearly claimed her life, her spirit remained resilient, buoyed by the love surrounding her.

Elizabeth bustled around the kitchen, preparing a hearty meal for the family. She occasionally glanced over at Tiffany, her eyes filled with concern and affection.

As the room filled with the scent of pine and cinnamon, Bill leaned over to Tiffany, planting a fond kiss on her lips.

"You're the brightest light in our lives, Tiff," he whispered, his voice thick with emotion.

She smiled weakly, her eyes shimmering with tears of gratitude. Though she could not actively participate in decorating the tree, she felt an overwhelming sense of peace and contentment. Her family was together, celebrating the season of love and healing.

CHAPTER THIRTY-FOUR

CHRISTMAS EVE ARRIVED, A SPLENDID sunny California day. Tiffany's step-dad, Chase, flew down to join the family celebration. He was dismayed to see her in such a feeble condition. Over the years, he had grown to love her dearly and admire her resilience after her father had died. His heart was heavy with sadness for her suffering.

There was a knock at the front door. "Who is it?" Bill asked.

"Your security guard, Alex. I have a delivery for you."

Alex held a huge bouquet of roses. "I checked them carefully."

"Thank you!" Bill said. "Merry Christmas."

"Sweetheart," Bill called, "a present for you!"

Tiffany gasped as Bill set it on the coffee table, "Fire and Ice, my favorite!"

"Twenty-five of them for the twenty-five Christmases we've had together!"

He carefully removed a rose from the cluster, handing it to Tiffany.

"They're gorgeous! Thank you," she grasped it with a tremor in her hand.

Their delicate, sweet floral fragrance filled her with delight, lighting her face with pleasure.

Elizabeth prepared their traditional Christmas Eve ham dinner. It was slow-cooked, succulent, and juicy with a glaze to knock your socks off. The glaze consisted of brown sugar, pineapple juice, honey, mustard, thyme, rosemary, cinnamon, and cloves. It was a holiday classic, sweet, tangy, and savory.

After dinner, Bill and Chase cleaned the kitchen while Tiffany and Elizabeth rested by the fire, sipping eggnog. When they were all settled in the living room, Chase read the Christmas story of the birth of Jesus from the book of Luke in the Bible. Then, they opened the few presents that were under the tree.

The festive occasion was tempered by the inescapable menace hanging over their heads. It threatened to consume them, foreshadowing evil and more tragic developments. Danger loomed on the horizon.

On Christmas morning, Sidney and Austin were up early. They served everyone steaming Colombian coffee with croissants as they relaxed in their pajamas and robes. Then, they prepared a delectable brunch, breakfast casserole. The recipe had been passed down through the family generations. Austin preheated the oven to 400 degrees. He put a cube of butter into a thirteen-by-nine-inch pan and placed it in the oven. Sidney beat ten eggs in a large mixer. Next, they added and mixed, one pint of cottage cheese, one pound of Monterey/Jack/Colby grated cheese, one to two cups of diced ham, one-half cup of flour, one-half teaspoon of baking powder, three dashes of Tabasco, and the melted butter from the pan in the oven. They poured the mixture into the warm pan and baked at 400 degrees for fifteen minutes. Last, Sidney changed the oven temperature to 350 degrees for about thirty minutes until a toothpick stuck in the middle came out clean.

They sat around the dining room table, enjoying Mimosas, coffee, egg casserole, left-over ham, and more croissants.

It was a quiet day of visiting and munching on Christmas cookies. Later, Elizabeth made addictive, warm, and melty ham and cheese sliders.

To complete the meal, she partnered them with creamy, tomato basil soup. Tiffany's family was grateful to be alive, celebrating with her parents. There was so much to be thankful for.

Annabelle called to wish Tiffany and the family a Merry Christmas. She invited her to lunch at her home, thinking the view and fresh ocean breezes would do her good. Annabelle picked her up, loading the wheelchair in the back of the car. Tiffany walked as much as possible around the house but tired easily.

During the drive, they caught up on their Christmas get-togethers, discussing the family that came and all the delicious food they ate. Tiffany marveled at the breathtaking panoramic view as they approached Annabelle's and Grayson's luxurious mansion, perched atop a cliff on the beach. The golden rays of the morning sun gently kissed the horizon. Whisps of cotton candy clouds lazily drifted across the expanse, casting whimsical shadows on the azure waters of the Pacific Ocean below.

They entered the sprawling mansion. Tiffany remembered the opulent architectural details from the New Year's Eve party last year, but it had been nighttime. Expansive floor-to-ceiling windows framed the stunning vista. From the comfort of the living room, she could see the majestic beauty of the ocean stretching endlessly into the distance.

"Let's go for a walk outside. You will appreciate the gardens and views," Annabelle suggested.

"I would love that! Would you mind if we take the wheelchair?"

"Not at all! I'll put a blanket around you. There's a cool breeze off the water."

The lush, manicured gardens surrounded the mansion. Annabelle pushed Tiffany to a viewpoint where she could see vibrant Bougainvillea cascading down the cliffside. Palms swayed gently in the breeze, their fronds rustling softly. Exotic flowers perfumed the air with their sweet fragrance.

Annabelle pushed the wheelchair onto the grass and down the slope to the cliff's edge. The tide was out. Tiffany could see the surfers carve graceful arcs across the waves. Seagulls glided effortlessly, their plaintive cries echoing in the distance.

"Can you see the Santa Monica Pier?" Annabelle asked, pushing the wheelchair closer to the edge of the cliff.

"Please, no closer! Heights make me nervous!"

From this vantage point, time seemed to stand still. The rhythmic melody of the waves crashing serenaded the senses.

Tiffany's heart lurched and her hands began to sweat as Annabelle moved the wheelchair closer for a better view.

A deep voice called out behind them, "Hi ladies! Enjoying the view?"

Annabelle startled, "Yes, Darling! We were going to head back for lunch!"

"You're too close to the edge!" he exclaimed, alarmed, taking hold of the wheelchair and moving it back.

"We wanted to see the Santa Monica Pier!"

Grayson pushed the wheelchair up the slope, "How are you doing, Tiffany?"

"I'm getting stronger and stronger every day!"

"We were horrified to hear what happened to you! We're so sorry!"

"Yes, it has been pretty terrifying for my family!"

Grayson stayed for lunch with the ladies, attending to Tiffany's every need. Annabelle reluctantly drove her home, wanting her to stay longer, but she was worn out. Unknown to Annabelle, Grayson followed at a distance, assuring Tiffany got home safely.

CHAPTER THIRTY-FIVE

New Year's Eve was quiet at Tiffany's and Bill's home. The kids were at friends for the evening. Elizabeth and Chase flew home to Seattle, preparing to return to their jobs. Bill drew Tiffany close as they cuddled on the couch, watching New Year's Eve celebrations around the world on TV. They sipped Sanoma Pinot Noir with their salty, buttery popcorn. He reached over, turning her face toward his. Her lips brushed his, softly, delicately, like butterfly wings, just long enough that he inhaled her breath. He felt the warmth of her skin. Love washed over him at her sweetness. She laid her head on his shoulder, feeling a deep closeness and trust. Even as her heart rate increased, she felt relaxed and secure, enjoying the intimacy of their love for each other.

An hour's drive away, Isaiah and George were halfway through their twelve-pack of beer. They had nothing to do tonight and New Year's Day except sit back in their recliners, watch football, nap, and down some more beers.

"I don't understand what happened!" Isaiah fumed. "The amount of poison you put in that cleaning solution should have killed her!"

"That's one tough lady!" George observed.

"This time none of them will get away! I have an ironclad plan!"

"What's that?"

"We are going to celebrate Martin Luther King, Jr. Day! Early in the morning, while they are still asleep, we're going to pour gas around their house and set it on fire! If they try to escape, they'll be burned! They can suffer like Cameron! He will never be the same!"

"You will finally have your revenge!"

"It will be sweet!"

New Year's Day was on a Saturday, so Tiffany had another day to rest before returning to school. Carl picked her up early Monday morning. It broke his heart to see the usual spring missing in her step! He blamed himself for not thinking of poison! Nothing would get by him now!

The next two weeks were challenging. Tiffany sat to do her teaching. Carl helped but she was exhausted by the end of the day. She looked forward to the long holiday weekend, resting an extra day.

It was Sunday night, January 16, 1994. Tiffany and her family went to bed, glad that they would be able to sleep longer the next morning since it was the Martin Luther King Jr. holiday. But it was not to be!

Tiffany and her family were nestled in bed during the early hours of January 17. An unknown fault under Northridge ruptured and briefly thrust the earth's crust violently upward. They were thrown out of their beds. The staggering 6.7 Richter magnitude earthquake shook for more than twenty seconds. It was 4:31 a.m.

The next minutes were a nightmarish frenzy. Tiffany could hear crashing, things shattering, groans, and booms. Outside, on their back property line, the electric wires were slapping together, creating huge sparks and flashes of light. When the ground ceased the tumultuous process of uplifting and twisting, all the power went out. It was deathly quiet.

"Everyone, find some shoes and get out of the house!" Bill yelled. "There's probably broken glass everywhere!"

Stunned and disoriented, it was impossible to find emergency flash-lights, let alone shoes! The furniture was askew. The floor was ankle-deep in belongings.

"Sidney, Austin, are you okay?"

"Yes!" they yelled, groping around in the dark, trying to find shoes.

"Bill, please help me!" Tiffany moaned.

She had landed on the floor in the initial thrust. The dresser had fallen on top of her.

"Austin, get to the gas main and shut it off! I'm helping your mom!" Bill ordered.

That was not an easy job for Austin. His bed had traveled across the room, jamming up against his door. He struggled in the pitch dark, pushing it over, trying to get out. He made it out and found the front door. The security guard was coming into the house to help everyone get outside. Austin explained what he needed to do. With the guard's flashlight, they made their way around the side of the house to the gas main. Grabbing the wrench hanging on the pipe, Austin shut off the gas line.

He rendezvoused with Sidney and the security guard in the front yard.

"Where's your mom and dad?" he asked.

"My dad said he was helping her."

"I'll go help them!" he said, alarmed.

They walked out of the door as he approached, Tiffany supported by Bill's arm. She hugged them, grateful to see everyone safe. The darkness was oppressive. They could hear explosions and see fires at a distance. The air smelled nauseating, a mixture of natural gas and smoke. Homes suddenly burst into flames, lighting up the dark sky.

Tiffany noticed Sidney was holding her arm, "Did you hurt your arm?"

"I think I hit my lamp when I was thrown out of bed."

The security guard turned on his flashlight, "Let me take a look. You have a cut, probably from your lamp. I'll get a bandage for you from my car."

As dawn broke, Tiffany's family was unaware that they had experienced the most damaging earthquake to strike the United States since the San Francisco quake of 1906! Homes, apartment buildings, and even hospitals collapsed all over the San Fernando Valley. They stood as if frozen in time in their front yard, shivering in the crisp morning air, only in their pajamas. Gas explosions were unnerving as hundreds of gas and water mains broke. The security guard decided to try to get home to check on his family.

They walked around the back of the house. Part of their concrete block wall was crumbled. Bricks littered the patio from the broken fireplace chimney. Most of the water had sloshed out of the swimming pool. The patio furniture and debris were scattered about the yard.

They huddled together as another strong aftershock hit, sending them to the ground. A house down the block exploded into flames. Smoke billowed overhead, blocking the rising sun.

"What are we going to do?" Austin's voice shook as he shivered.

"I'll go inside and see if it's safe for us to get dressed. We'll take it one minute at a time!"

Bill disappeared into the house while they waited to hear what he had found. In fifteen minutes he returned, his face drawn with concern.

"We have no power, running water, or phone service so we are completely cut off!" Bill reported.

"Our families are going to be worried!" exclaimed Sidney.

"We'll communicate with them as soon as possible!" assured Tiffany.

"You are going to be shocked when you walk in the door! Get dressed quickly, and get back and stay outside until these aftershocks are less severe!"

"I need to go to the bathroom!" said Sidney.

"There's no water in the toilets. Everyone can use the bathrooms. We'll flush them later with the water left in the pool."

They apprehensively approached the house. The back door hung askew, its frame shifted by the earthquake's force. Entering their home, they were struck by dismay. The kitchen, once a hub of activity and warmth, was in chaos. Dishes lay shattered on the floor, while cabinet doors swung open. The fridge had toppled over with food spilled across the linoleum.

They carefully walked into the living room. Furniture lay overturned, and lamps lay smashed into pieces. Cracks zigzagged across the walls like spider webs. Stepping into the bedrooms, closets had emptied, clothes and shoes mingled with broken glass and fallen plaster. They looked through the door going into the garage. Tiffany's car was buried in Christmas decorations and storage items that had flown off the shelves.

Suddenly, the ground began to shake again. Windows rattled and walls and floors creaked. They dropped to the rolling floor, covering their heads.

When it settled down, Bill ordered gravely, "Get dressed. Meet in the front yard!"

On the way out, Tiffany grabbed some intact bowls off the kitchen floor, spoons, and a box of cereal. She found the carton of milk under the table, still sealed.

They sat on the grass sharing the cereal. The mood was solemn. Their sense of safety and security was shattered again, along with their home. Yet, amid the devastation, they were profoundly relieved they had survived. They had not yet come to terms with the magnitude of the disaster that had struck their lives. Another aftershock caused the earth to tremble beneath them.

CHAPTER THIRTY-SIX

ONLY A FEW HOURS BEFORE, Tiffany's family had woken up on the floor of their bedrooms in the total darkness of the early morning. Bill took charge, rallying the family to assess the damage and formulate a plan. They decided to begin the task of clearing out debris. Austin and Sidney took two large garbage cans into the living room. They swept up the broken items and rubble, dumping them into the cans.

"This is why we hold on to things lightly," Bill commented as he tossed Tiffany's favorite lamp.

Once the house was cleared enough to walk around, Bill and Austin stacked the bricks, that had fallen from the fireplace, in a pile on the patio. Tiffany and Sidney scoured the kitchen, salvaging whatever food remained useable from the fridge and cupboards. They carefully inventoried their resources, noting what they could consume in the coming days.

Realizing their home was unsafe, they hauled out the camping equipment. The strong aftershocks were unnerving. They pitched the tents in the front yard, blowing up the air mattresses for the sleeping bags. There was a camp table that unfolded. They found the folding chairs in the chaos of the garage and blankets for the cool evening. The propane stove was set up along with a set of pots and pans.

Their neighbors across the street had a recreation vehicle parked in their driveway. They came over and offered to share food and water. Their generator for the RV would keep some food items cold for a while. Other neighbors joined in to share whatever food and water they had in storage. The sudden catastrophic events put all of them in survival mode. The stress was unrelenting and the future uncertain.

The day went by quickly with all the work they had done. Lighting the two-burner camp stove, they warmed up cans of Chili, sprinkling grated cheese on top, and Fritos, topping it with a dollop of sour cream. Tiffany found a supply of paper plates, bowls, and cups. It would be hard to clean up with no water.

"Guess what I found in our bedroom," Tiffany said, "a grapefruit from the fridge at the opposite end of the house!"

They all laughed, imagining the path the grapefruit had to take. It was the first attempt at levity in their tragic day.

Once the sun set, there was not much to do and they were exhausted. They crawled into their sleeping bags, fully clothed, and armed with flash-lights. Who knew what dangers the night might bring? It was difficult to get sleep between the aftershocks. It was a long worrisome night.

The rising sun warmed the morning air, still smelling burnt and sickening. The constant sound of sirens and helicopters reminded them why they were sleeping in tents in their yard.

Bill had always loved cooking breakfast. They had put their remaining ice in the cooler so he had eggs to make omelets. First, he cooked up some bacon, mushrooms, and onions. He whipped the eggs with a fork, cooked them, and filled them with shredded cheddar, onions, mushrooms, bacon, and sour cream. They finished up the last of the orange juice. He put the old campfire coffee pot on a burner and perked a strong brew. Breakfast never tasted so good!

They decided to walk around their neighborhood to see what was happening. On the next block, they were astonished to see a house split in half!

They stood on the sidewalk, looking through the house to the backyard. They walked to the main street intersection that turned into their neighborhood. Geysers of water and flame shot up into the sky in the middle of the street! Unbelievable sights!

They continued walking up to the Kaiser health clinic and were shocked to see that the side of the building had slid off. It looked like a doll house where you could reach in and arrange the furniture in the rooms. Patients were being treated in the parking lot.

"Let's see if we can get your arm checked," suggested Tiffany.

They got in line. A nurse came along and asked what they needed care for.

She looked at the cut, "It doesn't need stitches. I'll treat it with an antibiotic and bandage it for you. Keep an eye on it. If it gets dark red marks, has fluid leaking out of it, increases in pain, or feels warm around it, come back."

"Thank you!" said Sidney.

They walked on to the park. It was a mass of people camped out. A tanker truck in the parking lot was filling up their water containers. Someone told Bill that their apartment building was uninhabitable. They did not have anywhere to stay.

Farther on, they heard a lot of noise, like a large group of people talking. They were in a long line down the block. In-N-Out Burger had brought in a generator and was serving free hamburgers. Bill decided they would get in line too. It was a long wait but they got a fresh, delicious hamburger each, a surprise!

On the walk back home, they saw homes that had burned down. They walked in silence, sobered by the scope of the devastation. As they neared their home, they saw the security guard waving to them. He brought two huge jugs of water. He also brought them up to date on the news.

The Los Angeles Mayor, Richard Riordan, declared a state of emergency. The National Guard activated one thousand five hundred troops to help earthquake victims. The Red Cross and Salvation Army were setting up shelters for people who lost their homes. President Bill Clinton declared Los Angeles County a national disaster area, so federal aid could be released. The death toll was rising and hundreds of people were injured. The Los Angeles United School District schools were closed. Freeways 5, 14, and 10 were severely damaged. A train derailed near Northridge. LAX flights were canceled. There was a city-wide curfew from dusk to dawn. It sounded overwhelming!

He also told them that his family was fine. Where he lived was better off, although they did not have any phone service yet. He had spent hours finding a way home, driving around damaged freeways and roads. Seeing that they were camped in the yard, he invited them to stay at his home. They thanked him but did not want to leave their home. They also very much appreciated him making the trip to bring them water.

The next day, a semi-truck drove up and parked in the middle of the block. A man hopped out, going door to door.

He saw Bill in the yard, "Would you folks like to have a shower?"

Bill looked at the truck. It had doors along the side and steps that could be pulled down. He had never seen a shower truck before!

"We would love to!"

They showered and washed their hair, feeling refreshed and grateful.

It was a week before Tiffany went back to school. The schools in the San Fernando Valley sustained more damage, so it took much longer before Sidney and Austin could return to classes. Bill's office building was "red-tagged" as unsafe to enter, so they set up workspaces in one of their health clinics. It would be a long time before life resembled normalcy!

CHAPTER THIRTY-SEVEN

T IFFANY AND HER FAMILY SAT in the folding chairs out on their front lawn. It was a comfortable sixty-seven-degree day. A gentle breeze was playing with the leaves and twigs. Tiffany and Bill discussed trying to sleep in the house that night. The kids still freaked out at every aftershock, so it would be a while before they braved it.

A car drove into their driveway. Out stepped Detective Harris. He greeted everyone, pulled up a chair, and listened to their earthquake stories. Then, he described his experience which was similar to theirs. He did not have power, water, or phone service either. The police headquarters did, so he spent his time hanging out there. Since the earthquake, they had been working night and day anyway.

"I have something to tell you," Harris said, a serious note in his voice. Early Monday morning, Isaiah and George drove to the San Fernando Valley. They took the exit that would get them to Reseda Boulevard. The earthquake struck, thrusting upward as they went under the overpass, causing part of it to crumble. A piece of concrete fell onto their car crushing Isaiah. It rested at an angle, allowing George to crawl out. He was critically wounded. Eventually, he was picked up by an aid car and taken to a hospital. He asked for me, so the staff called to let me know. When I got there, George was dying."

Tiffany's eyebrows raised, causing wrinkles across her forehead. She was wide-eyed, amazed at the story Harris was relating. They were all astounded!

"I've only just begun," Harris stated. "You better get comfortable."

"George wanted to confess what Isaiah and he had done to you and Mateo. I recorded it. He said that when he put the skull on your car, it was only to frighten you, causing you anxiety and stress. The blood was red paint that he had found in a storage closet. It had been used in the murals painted on the walls of Leo Politi.

"When you left your purse in the classroom when you went on the field trip to the beach, he copied your home address from your driver's license. He also had copies made of your keys.

He felt awful when he slashed the heads of your Djembe drums! His brother was putting pressure on him. He was loyal to Isaiah who looked out for him when their parents died. Throughout his confession, he was extremely remorseful.

"George was upset with what Isaiah did to Austin. He did not know that Isaiah was going to run Austin down until he sped up the car. He yelled at him but Isaiah wouldn't stop. He had become obsessed with hate, seeing Cameron suffer. There was no reasoning with him.

"When Isaiah pushed Marcela over the edge of the ravine at her first communion celebration in the park, he borrowed a dog from a friend. He was also consumed with hatred toward Mateo and his cousins for attacking his sons during the riot as they tried to get Tiffany out of her car.

"Isaiah had a gun hidden in his office in the gym at school. If he stood on his desk and moved a ceiling tile over, he could reach up to get it. One day he brought it home. They drove to Sidney and Austin's school, waiting for classes to end for the day. Then, they followed them. Isaiah drove. He gave the gun to George and had him sit in the back seat with the window down. When there was an opportunity, he was to shoot Sidney. George said he purposely missed. He accidentally nicked her arm with the movement of the cars.

"George was afraid of what might happen during the home invasion. He had Isaiah take care of the guard so he could make sure Bill didn't get hurt. They wore ski masks, preventing anyone from recognizing them. Tiffany was expected to be home. George was thankful that she wasn't. Isaiah had lost control, becoming angry and violent.

"At Mateo's construction site, they loosened the brackets on the scaffolding and greased the boards. Isaiah was disappointed that Mateo's cousin survived the fall. He hadn't cared who fell. The plan was to hurt Mateo's business, causing him inconvenience, money losses, and delays.

Isaiah's hatred of Tiffany consumed him to the point of planning her death by poison. He never knew George had diluted it in the cleaning solution, hoping she would only get a little sick. Even then, he regretted that he had not diluted it even more. He wished he had stood up to his brother who had crossed the line.

"The plan, in the early morning hours of January 17, was to pour gasoline along the walls of Tiffany's house. That way, if they woke up in time and tried to escape, they would be burned. George planned to leave a gap, free from gasoline, along the house where they could get out unharmed. They had filled gas cans and were on the way when the earthquake occurred. This was Isaiah's vengeance for Cameron's burns. The earthquake foiled their plans. George grieved the loss of his brother, regretting his violent death!"

They listened to Harris in disbelief, appalled at the depth of Isaiah's hatred. Emotions of dismay and horror coursed through them as they tried to assimilate the death-bed confession.

"George wrote you a letter, Tiffany," Harris continued. "He left it above a ceiling tile in the maintenance storage room at Leo Politi. Something else was there too! A beautiful ruby necklace!"

"I don't believe it!" Tiffany jumped up, giving Bill a big hug.

She whipped around, "Wait! You never mentioned Neville!"

"George did not think Isaiah killed Neville. It may have been someone from a crime he solved. There's a particularly bitter man who got out of jail just before Neville was shot. We are going to interview him and see if he has an alibi. Detectives get a lot of death threats!"

"Will we need to have security guards?" asked Bill.

"No, you're safe now! I'll let Carl know."

"Carl is part of our family! We've been through so much trauma together. We're grateful to him for his unwavering care and support!"

Bill continued, "We want to thank you, Harris, for not giving up! We may have never known the truth if George hadn't asked for you!"

"It's been a pleasure for me!" responded Detective Harris. "It was frustrating knowing that I had connected the dots but couldn't find the evidence to prove it in court!"

Harris looked at Tiffany's expectant expression, "I have the letter and the ruby necklace in my car. I'll get them."

He handed her an envelope and a velvet box. With trembling hands, Tiffany opened the box. Her eyes filled with tears as she gently draped the necklace over her hand. The rubies sparkled like ocean flowers, their intense red hue symbolizing happiness, passion, and protection from all perils. The delicate necklace had special meaning to Bill and Tiffany—enduring love, survival, resilience, solidarity, and loyalty.

After Harris left, Tiffany opened the letter and read it silently to herself.

"Dear Tiffany,

I want to tell you how sorry I am for all the pain my brother and I caused you and your family. I regret not standing up to Isaiah but I owed him so much.

I want to ask for your forgiveness.

I grew to love you,

George

P.S. I saved your necklace for you!"

Tiffany shared the letter with her family.

She and Bill slept in their bed that night, locked in each other's arms.

CHAPTER THIRTY-EIGHT

O VER THE NEXT FEW WEEKS, Tiffany's family cleaned up their house so it was livable. They applied for funds to repair the earthquake damage. It would be months for that to be approved. Meanwhile, FEMA, the Federal Emergency Management Agency, gave them one thousand dollars for supplies and food. Sidney and Austin finally moved back into their bedrooms, storing away the tents and camping equipment. Tiffany's and Bill's families were relieved to hear from them when phone service was restored. Life was not the old normal yet. The gas company was slowly getting houses hooked up, so they cooked in the crock pot and microwave. Aftershocks frequently rolled through the area, keeping them on edge. Their lives still seemed to be in an upheaval.

Tiffany felt strange returning to school in February without Carl. His presence had given her a sense of security. She had to drive a different route to get on the freeway since the on-ramp, which she usually used, collapsed during the earthquake. Her students cheered her heart with their warmth, love, and enthusiasm. They were making significant strides in their reading skills. Drumming circle time was fun as they developed a varied repertoire of complicated rhythms. Their March break came all too soon. Tiffany would use that time to gain back more physical and emotional strength and process the trauma from the poisoning, earthquake, and George's death-bed confession. April and May would be the last two months of the first-grade year.

The sun gently peeked through the curtains, painting the room with soft hues of gold and amber. Bill woke from his slumber, feeling the warmth of Tiffany's presence beside him. He gazed at her peaceful face, illuminated by the morning light, and smiled.

With tender care, he leaned in close, brushing aside a stray lock of hair that had fallen across her forehead. His lips met hers in a lingering kiss, filled with love and affection. It was a kiss that spoke volumes, conveying all his unspoken words of devotion and appreciation.

As they parted, he caressed her cheek, his eyes reflected the depth of his feelings. "I'll miss you," he whispered, his voice a mix of longing and anticipation.

She returned his affectionate gaze, her eyes sparkling with warmth and understanding. "I'll be counting the minutes until you're back," she replied.

With one final embrace, they reluctantly released each other, knowing that duty called. But in that brief moment shared between them, amidst the quiet beauty of the morning, they found solace in the knowledge that their love would carry them through the day ahead.

Bill left for work and Sidney and Austin left for school. Tiffany had completed planning for dinner and did some weeding in the flower beds. The cool, refreshing pool was calling her. She dove in swimming slow and steady laps, relaxing her body and mind.

"Hi there," a voice called.

Annabelle walked around the corner of the house.

"Annabelle, what a wonderful surprise!" Tiffany exclaimed, getting out of the pool and reaching for her towel.

Annabelle aggressively walked over, planting herself with her back to the pool, her jaw clenched, glaring at Tiffany.

"Annabelle, what's wrong?" Tiffany asked, unnerved, putting on her robe.

From behind her back, Annabelle brought out a gun, leveling it at Tiffany's chest, "The day has finally come when you will not be able to escape. Since you walked into our company, Grayson has been in love with you! I saw how he looked at you! He was always making an excuse to call you into his office! He was supposedly "training" you! He talks about you all the time! He insisted on taking the drums over to your school!"

"But, Annabelle, there was never . . ."

"Shut up! I saw how he looked at you at the New Year's Eve Party! He couldn't wait to hold you close on that dance floor, taking you around the corner where Bill and I couldn't see you!"

"Annabelle, we weren't . . ."

"Shut up, Bitch! I killed Neville! He was getting too close to discovering who was harassing you and putting your life in danger! I wanted whomever it was to do the job for me but you're still here! Someone wanted revenge for Cameron! They failed!"

"Annabelle, I thought we were . . ."

"I kept pretending to be your friend to get information on what was being discovered in the investigations! I was hoping your wheelchair would accidentally roll off the edge of the cliff, but Grayson came to your rescue! If you are dead, Grayson will love me again!"

"Annabelle, you don't have to . . ."

"I said, 'Shut up, Bitch!' " she yelled, steadying her grip on the gun with both hands, finger on the trigger. She aimed, "Say goodbye, Tiffany!"

Tiffany dove onto the seating area rug. There was a sharp, explosive "POP!" A bullet punched its way through Annabelle's neck, causing a gaping hole in its wake that quickly filled with blood. Her gun dropped with a clatter onto the patio. Annabelle toppled backward into the pool with a smack on the surface, like a belly flop! Tiffany screamed! A red ribbon of blood floated to the top!

Tiffany jumped up, seeing Grayson, gun in hand, running toward the pool. They both jumped in, pulling Annabelle's unresponsive body onto the pool deck. They sat by her, panting for breath.

Grayson yelled at Tiffany, "Call an ambulance!" He grabbed a towel, holding it tightly against Annabelle's neck wound.

Within minutes the paramedics arrived, sadly announcing that she was dead. They called the police, as Grayson, ashen and shaking, cradled her head in his lap.

"We had a terrible fight!" Grayson exclaimed, tears coursing down his grief-stricken face, his body racked with sobs. She was yelling and accusing me of scenarios she had imagined. She was consumed with jealousy! She was irrational and wouldn't listen to me! She stormed off, saying she was going to kill you! I followed because she had become so violent! I'm so sorry! This is all my fault!"

Tiffany called Bill, struggling to keep herself under control as tears blurred her vision. She assured him she was fine. The police were handling things.

"Drive home safely!" Tiffany urged.

"Stay calm, Sweetheart! I'll be right there! I love you, Tiff!" Bill was gone, already running to the exit.

Terror ripped through Bill's heart as he witnessed the scene on his back patio. The Medical Examiner was investigating the cause and circumstances of the sudden, violent death of Annabelle. There was no need for an autopsy to be performed. The cause of death was established, and Grayson confessed to the shooting. He called the family funeral home to pick up her body. The police took him in for a statement. They were still investigating, collecting evidence.

Bill held Tiffany, trembling as she wept at the brutal betrayal and death of her friend. She felt shocked and angry! How could she not have known? She trusted and loved Annabelle! This was more than hurt! Grievous sorrow filled Tiffany's heart to think Annabelle had worn a mask, deceiving her. Annabelle was leading a life of quiet desperation, delusional, believing her distorted spin on things. Grayson did love Annabelle!

CHAPTER THIRTY-NINE

Tiffany's family was suffering the loss of Annabelle. Bill called the counselor who had helped them recover from the house invasion. They were working together through the healing process. It was not easy. Tiffany woke up with terrifying nightmares. Bill would hold her until she could fall back to sleep. The pool was drained and cleaned, but she would not go near it.

Bill did some research and then called a family meeting. When everyone was comfortable, he began.

"I've been doing a lot of thinking. We all survived rioting, personal and family attacks, and a major earthquake. We have shown strength and resilience. This would be a good time to begin a new chapter in our lives, a fresh start. I talked it over with my parents in Seattle. If we decide as a family to make a change, they have offered their home to us until we get established. They have a large house near Green Lake. Their primary bedroom suite is downstairs. There are three bedrooms and two bathrooms upstairs and a sitting loft. We would be very comfortable. Their location is close to the University of Washington where Sidney will be attending and where Shirley works at the medical center. For Austin, there's a good high school nearby with a well-known soccer program. Tiffany will have no problem getting a teaching job in the Seattle Public School District. Shirley already had an idea where I could apply for a job in the health-care field. Their house is within walking distance of Green Lake with a jogging and biking path, 2.8 miles around the lake. Nearby Woodland Park has tennis courts and play fields. A famous cafe is within a few blocks, Beth's Cafe. It serves a world-famous, hearty, delicious breakfast—an enormous twelve-egg omelet! If we decide to move, we will leave right after Sidney's graduation, the first week of June. That would give us the summer to get settled. Our realtor will get the repairs done on this house and get it sold. Then, we can look for a house to buy."

He hesitated, looking at their expressions, taking it all in. They asked questions and discussed the implications of moving or staying.

"Think about it overnight. We'll make a decision tomorrow!"

"I'm ready to vote on it now!" expressed Austin.

"Is everyone ready?" Bill asked.

They agreed. Bill got four pieces of paper.

"Write 'yes' if you want to move to Seattle and 'no' if you would like to stay here," he instructed.

It was unanimous! There were four "yes" votes to move to Seattle! The next two months would be a whirlwind of activity, getting ready to move.

Two months were left in Tiffany's school year. She did the testing required for her reading program. Moving was bittersweet, not having her students for second grade. The program had shown great success. It would be carried on after she left.

It was Tiffany's last day of school. Bill, Sidney, and Austin spent the day with her, enjoying the enthusiasm of her students. It was planned to have a classroom graduation with their parents and then a school-wide drum circle in the courtyard.

Graduation consisted of the usual arrival of the parents, showering Tiffany with gifts of appreciation. She graciously accepted their expressions of gratitude. The parents beamed with pride when their student was honored for his hard work and accomplishments.

That afternoon at Leo Politi Elementary School, anticipation buzzed through the air for the final Djembe drum circle. It had become a cherished event. Set against the backdrop of a community still healing from the scars of the Rodney King Los Angeles riots, this gathering held even deeper significance. It was a symbol of unity and resilience. Parents began to arrive with their families, their faces lit with excitement and anticipation. The drummers had taken their places, warming up under Mr. Lopez's direction. The courtyard filled with the rhythmic sound of the Djembe drums, their beats pulsating like the heartbeat of the neighborhood itself.

While not all students could be a part of the drumming circle, the others moved joyfully to the infectious rhythm. They weaved through the crowd in a dance of celebration and togetherness. Guests, too, joined, swept up in the energy of the moment.

There was a special group that moved beautifully together, bonded by shared experiences, loyalty, and trust. Tiffany had invited Carl and Detective Harris. They joined her, Bill, Sidney, and Austin. Kayla joined them with her boys, Jordan, Jasen, and Cameron. Martin was in the drumming circle. The owner, Mr. Kim, of the market where Jordan and Jasen worked, joined them. He had a fifth-grade son in the circle also. Mateo and Sara were part of the group, with Marcela in the drum circle.

As the afternoon performance progressed, the beats grew stronger, reverberating through the air and echoing off the surrounding buildings. The grand finale approached. The intensity of the music reached its peak.

Then, as if guided by an unseen force, the drummers shifted their rhythm. Their beats took on a new, solemn tone. A hush fell over the courtyard. At that moment, the entire neighborhood seemed to hold its breath, united by the simple, yet profound message resonating from the heart of the drum circle.

"Everyone, Gather Together in Peace!"

As the final notes faded, a sense of harmony and solidarity settled over the community, a reminder of the strength in coming together, and gathering in peace!

EPILOGUE

PART ONE: BLAZING

RODNEY KING RIOTS IN LOS ANGELES: TIMELINE

1991

March 3: Los Angeles Police officers beat, subdue, and arrest Rodney G. King. George Holliday, a resident of a nearby apartment, captures the beating on videotape and distributes it to CNN and other stations; it is soon seen around the world.

March 6: Police Chief Daryl F. Gates calls beating an "aberration." Community leaders call for Gates' resignation.

March 7: King is released after the district attorney announces there is not enough evidence to file criminal charges.

March 15: Four Los Angeles police officers—Sergeant Stacey C. Koon and officers Laurence M. Powell, Timothy E. Wind, and Theodore J. Briseno—are arraigned on felony charges stemming from the King beating.

March 16: A store security camera records the fatal shooting of fifteen-year-old Latasha Harlins, an African American girl, by Korean American Soon Ja Du in a South Los Angeles liquor store.

March 26: The four police officers charged in the King beating plead not guilty. Soon Ja Du is arraigned on one count of murder.

March 28: Records show that $11.3 million was paid to victims of police brutality by the city of Los Angeles in 1990 to resolve police abuse cases.

April 1: In response to the King beating, Mayor Tom Bradley appoints a commission, headed by former Deputy Secretary of State Warren Christopher, to investigate the Los Angeles Police Department.

April 4: The Los Angeles Police Commission places Gates on sixty-day leave.

April 5: The city council orders the reinstatement of Gates.

April 7: Gates takes disciplinary action against the four criminally charged officers. He fires probationary officer Timothy Wind and suspends the other three without pay.

May 10: A grand jury decides not to indict any of the nineteen officers who were bystanders at the beating. The police department later disciplines ten of them.

July 9: The Christopher Commission report is released; it suggests that Gates and the entire Police Commission step down.

July 10: Gates strips Assistant Chief David D. Dotson of his command after he complained openly of the chief's record in disciplining officers.

July 16: The Police Commission orders Gates to reinstate Dotson.

July 22: Gates announces he will retire in 1992.

July 23: The State Second District Court of Appeal orders the trial of the four LAPD officers moved out of Los Angeles County.

September 30: The prosecution in the Soon Ja Du–Latasha Harlins trial begins its case.

October 1: The police commission approves the vast majority of the 129 reform recommendations issued by the Christopher Commission.

October 11: The jury in Soon Ja Du's case returns a verdict: Du is found guilty of voluntary manslaughter.

November 6: The Los Angeles City Council approves spending $7.1 million to settle claims of police brutality and excessive force. Total payments for the year exceed $13 million.

November 15: Compton Superior Court Judge, Joyce Ann Karlin, sentences Soon Ja Du to five years of probation, four hundred hours of community service, and a five-hundred-dollar fine for the shooting death of Latasha Harlins. State Senator, Diane Watson, said, "This might be the time bomb that explodes."

November 26: Judge Stanley M. Weisberg chooses Simi Valley in neighboring Ventura County as the new venue for the trial of the officers charged in the King beating.

November 29: LAPD officers fatally shoot a Black man prompting a stand-off with more than one hundred residents in the Imperial Courts housing project in Watts.

1992

February 3: Pretrial motions begin in the trial of the four LAPD officers accused of beating Rodney King.

March 4: Opening arguments begin in the King trial. None of the twelve jurors is African American.

March 17: Prosecuting attorneys rest in the King trial.

April 3: Officer Briseno testified that King never posed a threat to the LAPD officers.

April 16: Willie L. Williams, the police commissioner in Philadelphia, is named to succeed Gates.

April 23: The jury begins deliberations in the King trial.

April 29: The jury returns not-guilty verdicts on all charges except one count of excessive force against Officer Powell; a mistrial is declared on that count alone. The verdict is carried live on television. Over two thousand people gather for a peaceful rally at First AME Church in South-Central Los Angeles.

Violence erupts. Police dispatch relayed reports of head wounds, vandalism, and burglary in an ever-widening radius. Reginald Denny is yanked from his truck cab and beaten unconscious at the intersection of Florence and Normandie; the incident is captured on video. Mayor Bradley declares a local emergency. Governor Pete Wilson calls out the National Guard. Fires break out over twenty-five blocks of central Los Angeles.

April 30: Bradley imposes a curfew for the entire city, restricts the sale of gasoline, and bans the sale of ammunition. The Justice Department announced that it will resume an investigation into possible civil rights violations in the King beating. Retail outlets are looted and/or burned in South Los Angeles, Koreatown, Hollywood, Mid-Wilshire, Watts, Westwood, Beverly Hills, Compton, Culver City, Hawthorne, Long Beach, Norwalk, and Pomona.

May 1: More than a thousand Korean Americans and others gather at a peace rally at Western Avenue and Wilshire Boulevard.

May 2: Clean-up crews hit the streets and volunteers truck food and clothing into the hardest-hit neighborhoods. Thirty thousand people march through Koreatown in support of beleaguered merchants, calling for peace between Korean Americans and Blacks. Mayor Bradley appoints Peter Ueberroth to head the Rebuild LA effort. President Bush declares Los Angeles a disaster area.

May 3: The *Los Angeles Times* reports 58 deaths; 2,383 injuries; more than 7,000 fire responses; 12,111 arrests; and 3,100 businesses damaged. The South Korean Foreign Ministry announced it would seek reparations for Korean American merchants who suffered damages during the unrest.

May 4: With troops guarding the streets, Los Angeles residents return to work and school. Twenty to forty thousand people have been put out of work because their places of business were looted or burned. In violation of long-standing policy, LAPD officers cooperate with the Immigration and Naturalization Service and begin arresting illegal immigrants suspected of riot-related crimes. Suspects are turned over to the INS for probable deportation.

May 6: President Bush receives a telegram from Representative Dana Rohrabacher (Republican, Huntington Beach) demanding quick deportation of illegal immigrants arrested during the riots.

May 8: Federal troops begin to pull out from Los Angeles. The Crips and Bloods (the two major gangs in Los Angeles) announce plans for a truce.

May 11: The Los Angeles Board of Police Commissioners appoints William H. Webster, former director of both the FBI and the CIA, to head a commission to study the LAPD's performance during the civil unrest.

May 12: Damian Williams, Antoine Miller, and Henry K. Watson are arrested for the beating of Reginald Denny on April 29. Gary Williams surrendered to the police later that day. They quickly become known as the L.A. Four.

May 16: Led by mayors of many of the nation's largest cities, tens of thousands of protesters demonstrate in the nation's capital demanding billions of federal dollars in vast urban aid.

May 19: A mistrial is declared in the case of a Compton police officer accused of fatally shooting two Samoan brothers a total of nineteen times, mostly in their backs. The jury was deadlocked nine to three in favor of acquittal.

May 21: Damian Williams, Henry K. Watson, and Antoine Miller are arraigned on thirty-three charges for offenses against thirteen motorists at the intersection of Florence and Normandie, including the attack on Reginald Denny. Bail is set at $580,000 for Williams, $500,000 for Watson, and $250,000 for Miller. None can post bail.

May 25: Korean grocers and leaders from the Bloods and Crips meet to discuss an alliance.

May 30: Chief Gates steps down. Willie Williams is sworn in.

July 7: Korean American protesters are pelted with office supplies tossed from city hall windows during the seventeenth day of protests over poor treatment from government officials since the riots.

September 24: Mayor Tom Bradley announces that he will not seek reelection the following June.

October 17: The Webster Commission reports that deficiencies in the LAPD leadership led to failure to respond quickly to April's civil unrest.

November 10: The trial date for defendants in the Reginald Denny beating is set for March 15, 1993.

November 17: The Black-Korean Alliance members vote to disband.

December 14: The intersection of Florence and Normandie flares again as the Free the L.A. Four Defense Committee protests at the site of Denny's beating.

1993

January 22: Superior Court Judge, John W. Ouderkirk, dismisses ten charges against the defendants in the L.A. Four cases, including charges of torture and aggravated mayhem. The charges of attempted murder stand.

February 3: The federal civil rights trial against the four police officers begins.

April 7: Judge Ouderkirk grants the defense in the Reginald Denny case additional time for preparation.

April 17: The verdicts are returned in the federal King civil rights trial. Officers Briseno and Wind are acquitted. Officer Powell and Sergeant Koon are found guilty of violating Rodney King's civil rights.

May 21: Peter Ueberroth resigns as cochairman of Rebuild L.A.

August 4: Sergeant Koon and Officer Powell are each sentenced to thirty-month prison terms.

August 19: The much-anticipated Reginald Denny beating trial begins in Los Angeles. Damian Williams, twenty, and Henry K. Watson, twenty-nine, are charged with a list of crimes including the attempted murder of Reginald Denny and others in South Central near the corner of Florence and Normandie.

September 28: Final arguments begin in the Denny trial.

October 11: Judge Ouderkirk dismisses a juror for "failing to deliberate as the law defines it." The juror is replaced with an alternate.

October 12: Judge Ouderkirk removes a second juror, who asked to be excused for personal reasons, from the jury in the Reginald Denny trial.

October 18: Damian Williams and Henry Keith Watson are acquitted of many counts against them.

December 7: Damian Williams was sentenced to a maximum of ten years in prison for attacks on Reginald Denny.

Photos of the rioting can be found at weaveofsuspense.com.

PART TWO: UPHEAVAL

NORTHRIDGE EARTHQUAKE: TIMELINE

A 6.7 magnitude earthquake struck underneath the San Fernando Valley community of Northridge, killing 57 people and causing $20 billion in damage: collapsed buildings and freeway overpasses, snapped water and gas lines, rampant fires, and landslides.

In the timeline below, follow along with the events as they unfolded:

1994

January 17

4:31 a.m.: A major earthquake strikes in Los Angeles.

4:37 a.m.: Fires, flooding, buildings down—widespread damage reported across Southern California.

4:39 a.m.: Freeways 5, 14, and 10 are severely damaged by the earthquake, the California Highway Patrol reports.

4:40 a.m.: Massive power outages are reported across L.A.

4:52 a.m.: Phone service is reported down in some areas.

4:56 a.m.: A train that may have been hauling hazardous materials derails near the Chatsworth/Northridge area.

5:17 a.m.: Quake-damaged scoreboard at Anaheim Stadium crushes upper-deck seating.

5:20 a.m.: Between 30 and 40 explosions are reported on Cal State Northridge campus.

5:38 a.m.: Federal Emergency Management Agency announces it will respond to the earthquake.

5:40 a.m.: Caltech reports that the magnitude—6.7 earthquake was centered in the northern San Fernando Valley area.

5:45 a.m.: Los Angeles Mayor, Richard Riordan, declares a state of emergency.

6:05 a.m.: All LAX flights are canceled; Metrolink service is shut down.

6:47 a.m.: As many as 50 structures are reported on fire.

6:50 a.m.: Hundreds of breaks in gas and water mains were reported. Parts of L.A. and Ventura counties are without running water or gas.

7 a.m.: Multiple people were found dead at a collapsed apartment building in the 9500 block of Reseda Blvd. in Northridge.

7:10 a.m.: All LAUSD schools are closed.

7:36 a.m.: Death caused by 14 Freeway collapse is identified as a law enforcement officer, fire spokesman says.

9:05 a.m.: Gov. Wilson declares a state of emergency and asks President Bill Clinton for federal aid.

9:10 a.m.: The National Guard activates its emergency operations centers to help earthquake victims.

9:18 a.m.: President Bill Clinton vows to help victims deal with the earthquake and its aftermath.

10:09 a.m.: Red Cross and Salvation Army set up shelters.

10:50 a.m.: Gov. Pete Wilson tours the Northridge earthquake area by helicopter.

12:02 p.m.: Power restored to nearly half of 1.4 million LADWP customers.

12:17 p.m.: Gov. Wilson dispatches 500 National Guard troops. More than 1,500 National Guard troops are expected within 24 hours.

1:00 p.m.: Tens of thousands of LA residents "may be homeless," Insurance Commissioner John Garamendi says.

1:10 p.m.: "Sporadic" looting leads to more than 25 arrests citywide, LAPD says.

2:08 p.m.: President Bill Clinton declares L.A. County a national disaster area, releasing federal relief for victims of the Northridge quake.

2:20 p.m.: Death toll rises to 29 and hundreds are injured as the search for survivors continues.

3:15 p.m.: Southern California Edison reports that power is restored to all but 150,000 homes and businesses.

5:20 p.m.: At least 14 people confirmed dead at Northridge Meadows Apartments.

5:50 p.m.: City-wide curfew in L.A. is in effect until dawn.

January 18

7:01 a.m.: Northridge Earthquake death toll rises to 33, including 15 at Northridge Meadows Apartments, officials say.

7:21 a.m.: LAUSD schools remain closed for the second day and nearly all schools in surrounding districts are closed. CSU Northridge, USC, and UCLA are among the colleges closed.

1:05 p.m.: Thousands of buildings in L.A. and Ventura counties reported damaged.

5:01 p.m.: Citywide curfew to be extended another day, LAPD Chief Willie Williams says.

7:15 p.m.: More than 800 people injured in Ventura County. Property damage is estimated at more than $400 million.

7:42 p.m.: Nearly 8,000 homes are still without water in Simi Valley.

January 19

6:01 a.m.: More than 500 were hospitalized, 2,300 treated and released Tuesday, hospital officials say.

7:33 a.m.: LAUSD schools remain closed for the third day in a row. At least 170 facilities are seriously damaged.

10:32 a.m.: President Bill Clinton arrives in Southern California.

2:36 p.m.: Los Angeles Department of Water and Power officials say three of four L.A. aqueducts were severed, but local water supply will last at least 7 to 10 days.

January 20

7:32 a.m.: About 36,000 LADWP customers are still without water this morning for the fourth day in a row.

10:32 a.m.: Electricity restored to all parts of L.A. except for 7,500 customers in the San Fernando Valley, utility officials say.

11:01 a.m.: Officials cancel dusk-to-dawn curfew.

2:06 p.m.: State will underwrite loans of up to $200,000 for small-business owners devastated by Northridge Earthquake, Gov. Wilson says.

January 21

7:15 a.m.: LAUSD schools remain closed for the fifth day in a row.

12:01 p.m.: Death toll rises to 55 people, officials say.

January 22

8:00 a.m.: LAUSD plans to reopen most schools. About 300 classrooms remain unsafe.

8:32 a.m.: Some 10,000 households in northwest San Fernando Valley remain without running water.

9:01 a.m.: Crews restore service to 40,000 homes and identify at least that many more that are still without gas, the Southern California Gas Company says.

10:05 a.m.: 236 military tents with a capacity for up to 7,340 people are expected to be in place at 7 Valley locations by nightfall.

1:00 p.m.: Federal government releases $283 million in earthquake aid, according to White House Press Secretary Dee Myers.

Photos of the earthquake can be found at weaveofsuspense.com